BEAUTY
FOR
ASHES

*" . . . to give unto them beauty for ashes,
the oil of joy for mourning . . ."*

— ISAIAH lxi. 3

Winifred Fortescue

ISIS
LARGE PRINT
Oxford, England

Copyright © 1948, Lady Fortescue

First published in Great Britain 1948
by William Blackwood & Sons Ltd

Published in Large Print 1997 by ISIS Publishing Ltd,
7 Centremead, Osney Mead, Oxford OX2 0ES,
by arrangement with Mrs Faith Grattan

British Library Cataloguing in Publication Data
Fortescue, Winifred, Lady 1888–1951
  Beauty for ashes. – Large print ed.
  1. Fortescue, Winifred, Lady, 1888–1951 2. Large type
books 3. England – Social life and customs 4. England –
Social conditions
  I. Title
942'.082'092

ISBN 0-7531-5032-8

Printed and bound by Hartnolls Ltd, Bodmin, Cornwall

BEAUTY FOR ASHES

Also available in this series:

Fred Archer	THE CUCKOO PEN
	THE DISTANT SCENE
	THE VILLAGE DOCTOR
H. E. Bates	FLYING BOMBS OVER ENGLAND
Brenda Bullock	A POCKET WITH A HOLE
William Cooper	FROM EARLY LIFE
Kathleen Dayus	HER PEOPLE
Denis Farrier	COUNTRY VET
Winifred Foley	NO PIPE DREAMS FOR FATHER
	BACK TO THE FOREST
Peggy Grayson	BUTTERCUP JILL
Jack Hargreaves	THE OLD COUNTRY
Mollie Harris	A KIND OF MAGIC
Angela Hewins	THE DILLEN
Elspeth Huxley	GALLIPOT EYES
Joan Mant	ALL MUCK, NO MEDALS
Brian P. Martin	TALES OF TIME AND TIDE
	TALES OF THE OLD COUNTRYMEN
Victoria Massey	ONE CHILD'S WAR
John Moore	PORTRAIT OF ELMBURY
	BRENSHAM VILLAGE
Phyllis Nicholson	COUNTRY BOUQUET
Gilda O'Neill	PULL NO MORE BINES
Valerie Porter	TALES OF THE OLD COUNTRY VETS
	TALES OF THE OLD WOODLANDERS
Sheila Stewart	LIFTING THE LATCH
Jean Stone	
and Louise Brodie	TALES OF THE OLD GARDENERS
Edward Storey	FEN BOY FIRST
	IN FEN COUNTRY HEAVEN
Nancy Thompson	AT THEIR DEPARTING
Marrie Walsh	AN IRISH COUNTRY CHILDHOOD
Roderick Wilkinson	MEMORIES OF MARYHILL

I dedicate this book to my readers all over the world.

WINIFRED FORTESCUE

INTRODUCTORY LETTER

DEAR READERS OF MY BOOKS,

I want each of you who has sent me such wonderful help and kind encouragement to read this letter as though it were written personally TO YOU, and to consider this book as YOURS.

It is a queer, much-interrupted book, begun and finished in England; isolated episodes scribbled in my studio of "Many Waters," in my caravan on the heights of Dartmoor or the woods of Hartland, in a little Adam house in London, a rambling Rectory in Hertfordshire, an old malt-house in Sussex, my little "Sunset House" in Provence, and the last chapters written in a divine little cottage in Berkshire, over two hundred years old, lent to me by a friend, who, loving France from girlhood, has decorated it in the style of early France — dim pastel shades of *bois de rose*, nattier blue, and celadon green, light and laughter everywhere. It is fitting that a book written about England and France should be finished in such a setting, among old French furniture, or in a garden filled with English roses and hollyhocks, with a view of distant woods and cornfields and cows grazing peacefully in the foreground.

When you read it you will realise the difficulties under

which it was written and understand the changes of tense; for sometimes I was writing in the present and sometimes in the past, and always my work for France must have precedence and the book be laid aside, sometimes for months. Now at last I have strung all the episodes together, and here it is, jerky and faulty I know, but written from the heart FOR YOU. It would not have been written at all had you not continually goaded my pencil into activity with your wonderful letters pleading with me to give you another book SOON and asking me, with real affection and solicitude, what had happened during those ghastly years of war to dear *Mademoiselle* (Elisabeth Starr), her little shadow-dog Squibs, to me and to Dominie, my little Blackness. Those of you who did not already know him and learn to love him through my books will very probably find a surfeit of Cocker Spaniel in these pages — but how could I describe my life through those years of war without speaking continually of him who was, and ever will be, part of me? Every letter of yours sends him loving messages, and because — now — they hurt, I had to write, through tears, one very sad chapter.

Perhaps when God took him to the Dogs' Paradise, as always, He knew best. Perhaps in that last weird wail to Heaven Dominie was saying good-bye and asking to be taken from me lest he cause me additional anguish in France. It would be like him to do that. How should I have fed my little man in a starving country? And how could Margharita and I have cared for him or played with him, overworked as we both were? He would have had no companions, because in the worst year of hunger in the South of France, 1943–44, when *Mademoiselle* died, the peasants killed and ate their dogs and cats. He would sorely have missed his early playmate, little Squibs.

His collar and lead hang in my tiny chapel built in the rock under "Sunset House," in the place where he always sat so quietly and so close to me while I said my prayers, and there is always a sprig of rosemary — for remembrance — tucked into its ring. Sometimes I think I see a little black shadow flit past me in the garden. Surely he is with me still? His Heaven would always be where I was.

Lastly, I want to thank YOU, personally, every man, woman, and child of you, who have given me personal help and who have made such generous sacrifices to send me money, clothes, comforts, and food for my children of Provence. I have always explained to them that these wonderful gifts came FROM YOU and had nothing to do with me, although I was granted the proud privilege of playing the part of *Maman Noël*. At first I called myself "The lone Crusader," but YOU soon changed all that by crusading with me. God bless you for all you have done — and are doing — for these pathetic children and for your loveliness to me. This book is my poor gift to you in return.

May I send each and all of you my love?

WINIFRED FORTESCUE.

AUGUST 1948.

A year has passed by since I handed the manuscript of YOUR book to my publisher. Only he and his long-suffering firm can know with what difficulties, vexatious restrictions and delays he has had to cope. But now he hopes to publish "Beauty for Ashes" in November, in time for Christmas.

During the past year supplies of all kinds have flowed gently into poor denuded France. The peasants are no longer hungry, for the rains came — with me — in 1945 and once again they could cultivate their land, keep a few hens and rabbits, and often a goat. But in the towns the poor suffer still, for prices are fantastic and they can hardly afford their meagre official rations, while the rich can buy every luxury in the Vile Black Market. Prices must be controlled and food distributed fairly. Then suffering will cease and France become the happy, smiling land we knew — and still love.

W.F.

CONTENTS

CHAPTER
ONE

Thrills of All Kinds

"Although it's war-time and there's only you and me to prepare a luncheon for four people, Kitty, I want our luncheon to be chic-erer than anyone else's in Sussex," I said to my little maid.

"Chic-erer, my lady?"

Kitty blinked at me like a puzzled owl through her horn-rimmed spectacles.

"Sir John's double comparative," I chuckled. "Smart, smarter, smarterer, smartest — just his own funny grammar, and *chic* is French for smart."

Kitty nodded sagely, not understanding in the least what her queer mistress was trying to explain, but, being sharp as a needle, immediately she seized upon a new word.

"Well, your ladyship, if my French beans aren't chic-erer than any cook's in Sussex it won't be my fault. That's why I wanted to slice 'em up to-night and get ahead for to-morrow."

"That's right, Kitty. No whiskers allowed — and isn't that little French vegetable knife you're using a pet for the purpose? I must be equally careful with the salted almonds when I blanch and skin them. Wasn't I lucky to find some? People love nibbling them all through a meal."

Kitty and I were sitting together in the cosy little kitchen of "Many Waters", my cottage in the woods. It had been abandoned by human beings for fifteen years, and the jackdaws had joyfully taken it for their own, until this refugee from France displaced them. When first I entered it I found skeletons of defunct jackdaws on the floors; the chimneys were stuffed with their nests. For months I waged war against the poor birds, who bitterly resented my intrusion, and, as fast as I hauled down the bushels of twigs they built into nests in MY tall chimneys, they set to work and filled them up again until, after a guest had been woken at dawn by their chatter and scrabblings in her chimney and the sudden appearance of an irate bird who fluttered down it into her room, and after one bad chimney fire, in desperation I hired men with tall ladders to cover the chimney-pots with wire. Even so, for years I heard furious swear-words being shouted down the chimney by the previous tenants of the cottage, who still strove to displace my protective wire — and sometimes succeeded.

For some time I had been comfortably installed in that little cottage set amid woods and waters in the loveliest spot in Sussex. At first I was alone — to the consternation of my family and friends, who considered such isolation to be dangerous — then with Kitty, a gallant local maiden, mercifully born without nerves. I was helping her now to prepare a little luncheon, planned for the morrow for the entertainment of my landlord, his mother and a guest of theirs; for I knew that with all the housework to do next day, Kitty would have no time for the final touches which are so important and make all the difference. I was squatting on a three-legged stool and, having peeled my almonds, was tossing them in butter and salt in a fryng-pan over the blue flame of a valiant little oil stove, as I prosed peacefully to Kitty intent on her beans, when —— WHOOOOOOoooooo CRRRRUUUMMPPP! The cottage shook, the doors flew open, crockery rattled in cupboards. A bomb.

I think it is to our credit that neither of us dropped a bean or an almond. After the first moment of surprised paralysis our eyes met, and we burst out laughing.

"Hullo, Jerry!" grinned Kitty. "Throwing 'em at *us* now, are you?" as she quietly selected another bean.

"It sounded as if it fell on the boat-house. Shall we go and look?" I said, after a pause during which we heard that ominous intermittent engine-throb pulse away into the distance.

"I think our windows would have gone bust if it had been as near as that, your ladyship," said Kitty. "But it was too near to be comfortable."

Outside the cottage there was utter peace. The little lakes glimmered mysteriously in the dim starlight. The boat-house stood intact. No yawning crater, no blur of rising smoke, no stench of burning mixed with the smell of damp leaf-mould, moss and trees in the woods. Only the freshness of the autumn night and running waters.

As a matter of fact that bomb fell upon and destroyed five cottages in the nearest village three miles away, but the wind blowing down our deep valley from that direction brought the blast of it to our doors. People from

3

the Big House, a quarter of a mile away, came rushing down the rock cliffs to see if we had been bombed to blazes; people from the main road ran through the woods to rescue us. The valley resounded with the shrill whistling of wardens, and the mule-bell hanging from its leather thongs outside my front door and the old Sussex horse-shoe posed on the door itself to serve as knocker were, for hours afterwards, kept busy summoning Kitty to know if we were still alive. So strange is the effect of bomb-blast in our ventriloquial valley. Kitty and I became quite apologetic for being still alive and well, and for causing all this unnecessary anxiety.

A few nights later we were awakened at midnight by a thunderous knocking at the door. I was walking in my rose garden in Provence at that moment, watering its wide border of English pinks and the thirsty tuber-roses and jasmine planted among my roses, talking happily with my beloved neighbour, *Mademoiselle* of the Château below my little "Sunset House", when so rudely dragged back to an England of ugly war. As I lit a candle I heard steps cross the hall and a subdued babel of voices talking urgently. Presently a knock at my door, and Kitty (happily for her, wearing a very pretty night-gown) appeared.

"Three A.R.P. wardens to see you, my lady," she announced.

"But Kitty! Tell them I'm in bed. I can't see them. What do they want?"

"They say there's an unexploded bomb in our valley," said Kitty. "They want us to get out of it. They won't go, and they say they must see your ladyship. One of them's a woman," she added, to comfort me.

"Then ask *her* if she will come up to my room," I said, and presently a slim tin-hatted lady with a buzz of fair hair and apologetic blue eyes entered my room.

"This is a very unconventional first call," she said, "but the Head Warden is convinced that an unexploded bomb fell near here and he is very anxious to evacuate you at once."

"At what hour is it supposed to have fallen?" I enquired.

"Soon after ten o'clock. We have been evacuating the gardeners' cottages on the estate."

"I had my wireless turned on until eleven and it registers every atmospheric disturbance even *too* faithfully, yet I heard nothing," I strove to reassure her, "and when that big bomb fell in the village three miles away everything in the cottage shook and our doors flew open. So this bomb *can't* have fallen near here, and you must please leave me in my warm bed. If my little maid is nervous, then please take her with you."

A voice from the gloom of the staircase:

"If you please, your ladyship, *I'd* rather stay in *my* warm bed." The undaunted Kitty!

Nevertheless it was some time before I could persuade those three wardens to leave us, and only succeeded by bribing them with sticks of glucose barley-sugar — glucose being said to be good for the nerves. My little fair-haired visitor descended the stairs very reluctantly, with her sugar-sticks, and rejoined the waiting men. Then Kitty and I once again composed ourselves for sleep.

Yet, when something dramatic really *did* happen in our vicinity, not a soul came near us for hours

5

afterwards. It happened thus-wise. The Hun was at that time busily blitzing London every night and, on his way thither, always passed over us. One night I had been hearing various strange noises for some hours, distant crrrrrrummpps and those strange wavering sounds made by the weaving hide-and-seek of aeroplanes in the skies. It was a cold clear night of early frost. Surely if I went out of doors I should see that very lovely tracery in the sky made by the icing of hot vapours from aeroplanes flying at a high altitude? I went out, and was not disappointed. Far up in the blue ether intrepid pilots were catching the stars in a white net of their own making.

So that I regretfully confess that both Kitty and I were "goofing" outside the cottage, doing exactly what every one had repeatedly been warned not to do during a raid, when — it happened ——.

There was a sudden terrifying screaming sound which sounded *very* near. I thought it must be a falling aeroplane, and then — well, I can only describe that shattering sound by saying that it was what I imagine the sudden end of the world might be if we hit a comet. A lurid glare stained the little lakes crimson, and columns of what I thought was smoke, but afterwards learned was tortured, blasted earth, hit the stars.

A land-mine on the other side of the nearest lake, but, thank God, no harm done, and far enough off not to ruin the lovely peaceful view from my windows. Another thing gave me keen satisfaction at that moment. I was pleased to note that the slight acceleration of the heart was greatly outbalanced by the thrill.

That night no one came down to look for bits of us. For

some hours I sat at the window of the little spare-room overlooking the woods and lakes in case the stick of petrol bombs which were dropped afterwards set fire to the surrounding woods I love so much, and at last, seeing no warning glow or cloud of smoke, I went back to my own room, undressed, got into bed and was soon asleep. But it must have been a very light sleep, for it was disturbed by a soft whistling outside my window. I switched on my electric torch and looked at my clock to find that it was two o'clock in the morning.

"The A.R.P. men have taken some time to realise where that land-mine dropped," I muttered to myself, turning off the light. After a while the whistling began again — the same little tune.

"That warden is no musician," I decided irritably, turning over on my pillow. But when that little insistent tune was whistled for the third time, I sat up in bed. *Could* it be possible that I was being serenaded — at the age of fifty-two? That was the second thrill of the night. I sprang out of bed and threw on the Alpine dressing-gown which covers me warmly from neck to heel, designed so lovingly by *Mademoiselle* to protect me from the icy cold of glaciers when we spent our holidays in the High Alps, and now very comforting in this English climate of ours. Then I drew aside the curtains and looked out. Below my window stood a strong stocky figure wearing a tin hat. I did not recognise my troubadour, and called to him:

"Who is it? What is it?"

A gruff voice replied: "It's Porter, my lady — Mrs. X's chauffeur. This isn't rightly my beat, but since I heard that bomb drop I've had your ladyship on me heart because I felt sure the thing fell hereabouts. I was afraid your ladyship might be buried in debris."

That man had walked three miles, after a long day's work, had braved the precipice and a wet walk through soggy woods, risking a fall into one of the lakes, to see if I was safe. Truly the world is full of wonderful people.

"Bless you, dear Porter," I said very gratefully. "And now won't you walk up those steps into my studio-bedroom — it is what is described as a 'bed-sitter' so I can receive you in it, and we'll brew some hot chocolate and smoke a cigarette."

Up those steps he came and, after some pressing, was persuaded to take off the tin hat from his grizzled head and to settle down cosily in my armchair. While I got busy with spirit-lamp and saucepan, brewing chocolate, he told me all about the search of the A.R.P. men for my bomb — in every locality but the right one — for the great rock cliffs of my valley had muffled the sound of the explosion. He had obeyed the orders of his warden and had searched in the directions indicated, but when the men were at last dismissed after a fruitless search and told they might now go home, he had decided to continue the search alone where his instinct told him the bomb had fallen. Then I was told all about Porter's son in the Air Force, and we discussed the conduct of the war, and when we had enjoyed our hot chocolate and a cigarette we said good night, and Porter tramped off into the woods.

The world *is* full of wonderful people.

The episode did not quite end there. Next day I was walking along the main road to fetch provisions when a car passed me. Suddenly it drew up and, as I approached it, Porter's employer looked out from the driver's seat. He was alone and his eyes were twinkling.

"I heard all about you and my old Porter last night," he said, with a chuckle.

"Wasn't it *divine* of him to come all that way and take all those risks to see if I was safe?" I countered.

"Very decent of him," nodded his employer. "The sequel will amuse you, I think. Apparently this morning the other A.R.P. men were boasting that during their search they had been welcomed into the kitchen of a certain noble earl, had been made much of and given beer, when suddenly old Porter reared up his head and said, with proud and crushing dignity:

"'*I* was asked into her ladyship's bedroom.'"

CHAPTER
TWO

Friends of All Ages

When I first found "Many Waters", although certain that I must at all costs live in it, I own that I was filled with misgivings about how furniture could be brought down the rock precipice and through the woods to its doors; for it had been a gamekeeper's cottage and there was no road to it. I had forgotten for the moment that if you want a thing furiously enough, somehow you are enabled to accomplished miracles, or to fire others with enough enthusiasm to accomplish them for you, and exactly this happened with the installation of my furniture; for of course, risking all, I took the cottage in this dream place. In another book* I have described the amusing agonies endured on that day of installation, mercifully — and for the first time in my experience of "moves" — a fine one. Our adventures on that occasion were as funny as any I have survived during removals and installations in England or Provence, and that is saying a good deal; but in this case the day ended triumphantly.

After that, fuel of every kind had somehow to be found and transported to the cottage — coal, logs, and paraffin

*Trampled Lilies, Wm Blackwood & Sons, Ltd.

for my lamps, since the little house had no electricity. But, as usual, I found gallant friends in the neighbourhood ready and willing to take the risks that I had taken. A coal merchant from a neighbouring village (not mine) sent his hefty son down another pathway through the woods in a small lorry. I believe it got both bogged and ditched before it eventually roared over the rough tussocky grass and down an uneven slope to the back of the cottage, where this brave lad unloaded my sacks of coal in quiet triumph. Even more gallant was the supplier of logs; the scion of an ancient Sussex family, soaked in the lore of his beloved county, his hardy spirit baked harder still by the sun of South Africa, where he had for some years striven to impart a fraction at least of his erudition to her young sons. Undeterred by his three-score years and ten he loaded heavy logs from his own estate into the most antique Ford car I had ever seen, the remnants of its chassis specially arranged for such excursions, and with his three little Cairns, known as "the three girls," sitting on the top of him, the youngest of them frantically yapping with excitement, his eyes gleaming with enjoyment, his grey hair blown on end by the wind, he thundered joyously down a steep track through the wood, in greatest danger from the shifting load of logs behind him, and from ancient brakes which might prove inadequate as he reached the edge of the lake. Braving concussion from logs on the head, and a watery grave, he delivered his timber, unloading it himself and stacking it in true forestry style.

There remained the problem of paraffin, but this proved easy of solution, for it was supplied by a superman living in our own village, a true Universal Provider with a wonderful brain, a keen sense of humour, a love of adventure and, I think, of the adventurous. To him I went and told my story. Knowing every corner of Sussex, through which he had wandered during a long life, he realised my difficulties, but also saw how they could be surmounted. A large empty fifty-gallon drum could be transported to the cottage, and small drums, full, carried down to fill it, until I had a good reserve. His van delivered goods to the cottages along the main road, so that my stores could be left at one of the gardeners' lodges of the estate whereon my wigwam was built. This unique storekeeper did not regard me as mad, but rather as superbly sane, to choose to live in this lovely, inaccessible place. It was I, not he, who foresaw difficulties; he skipped over them with the same agility that he skips over the boulders of this estate, when he can find time to roam it. Once during our interview I caught an appreciative gleam in his eyes as he surveyed this queer woman, though immediately those eyes were lowered and some practical suggestion made to hide that glimpse of his real self. But before we parted we twinkled at each other, and I knew that I had found a friend worth having. While talking of this surprising man afterwards to a friend living in the neighbourhood, she laughed and agreed that he was unique. "I have never known him fail to supply anything we wanted," she said. "Once I was getting up a Greek play and I wanted two good-looking young men to act as Greek gods. I couldn't find them anywhere, and then I suddenly thought of ringing up our friend. I told him of my difficulty and asked him if he knew of two such young men. At once he said he would make enquiries. Before I rang off he asked me if there was anything I wanted in the grocery line, as his van was calling next day. I said that I would much like a pound of Gorgonzola cheese, if he had any.

"'Certainly, madam,' he replied. 'Two Greek gods and one pound of Gorgonzola cheese' — and he delivered both my orders next day."

When paying me her first call, this same friend, a vital and glowing product of New Zealand, amused me very much by a recital of the war problems of her large establishment and her method of dealing with them. So much black-out material was needed to shroud this landmark at night that in the end she and the complete staff dyed black yards and yards of hessian — and, incidentally, themselves as well.

"And of course the first thing we did was to drain our lake — lakes are so visible from the air — OH! I'm SO sorry!" — and she clapped her hand over her laughing mouth as she remembered — too late — my local nickname, "The Lady of the Lake", because there were FIVE lakes near by.

My best allies and helpers during the moving-in proceedings — and ever since — were two of the gardeners and their dear wives, not to mention their children, living in twin lodges on the edge of the main road, one each side of the entrance to my right-of-way down the precipice and through the woods. Without their help life would indeed be difficult. From the first they received my stores and parcels, my letters and messages, and one or other of them brought them

13

down to me. Always one wife or the other came to cook and clean for me before I found my Kitty; the husbands set mouse-traps, battled with recalcitrant oil stoves, opened tins and bottles, chopped wood, scythed grass and nettles, and later, when winter set in, dug me out of the snow; besides dragging heavy baggage, oil-drums and other things up and down the precipice. The son and heir of one of them, a delightful blond imp of mischief, fetched twigs from the woods to light my fires, while his little sister gathered flowers from the hedges for my rooms. The son and heir of the other, a slender child with outsize eyes in a little sensitive face, constituted himself my chauffeur when at last a little wooden hut was erected half way up the precipice to house my cockle-shell car. My chauffeur had not then attained his seventh year, but he was always ready at the first hoot of my horn to rush forth and open the wooden gates which shut off the main road. When I came back from an excursion he was there again, and tore down the precipice ahead of me to open the garage door. Then he would climb on to the running-board and, with duster and polisher, rub the mud-spattered windows. It was a moment of great pride when first I taught him how to put in the contact-key before I started the engine, and the only thing that ever defeated him was the draping of it with a rug at night to keep out the cold. He would strive to fling the heavy rug over the bonnet, but always it flew back, completely enveloping his tiny person, which I then had to find beneath its voluminous folds and comfort with apples. His little sister was, later, my delight when in the spring she played beneath the windows while her mother was at work in my cottage. One day she made herself appear like a fashionable lady of my youth by stringing clusters of rhododendron blossoms, mauve and delicate pink, into the imitation of a long feather boa, which she wound elegantly around her little neck and shoulders.

Children, like fairies and gnomes and elves, haunted this enchanted place. Above me on the cliffs, a quarter of a mile away, fifty East End babies had been rescued from London, and now, with their L.C.C. teachers, inhabited the Big House while its owners were tucked away into minute lodges. Every day I would see — and hear — a procession of these tiny people, between the ages of two and five, trotting and tumbling down the grass slope in front of the cottage, clad in pointed woolly caps, and coats and mufflers of every brilliant hue. Their great excitement was to peer into my windows. For months, before I came, they had been told fairy stories about the little mysterious cottage in the woods, so that when for the first time they saw smoke actually rising from its chimneys, their excitement knew no bounds. I felt quite reluctant to shatter their dreams of a fairy inhabiting the cottage, so, for a long time, used to hide myself when they passed lest, peering in, they be scared to see this grey-curled old witch stirring her soup over the fire. However, one day they rounded a clump of azaleas just as I was going out of the front door, and to my delight, instead of showing fear and disappointment, they one and all rushed upon me squeaking out a chorus of questions — I had forgotten that they were the fearless children of London.

"'Ullo!"

"Oo are yer?"

"Wot's yer nime?"

"I'll pinch yer bot." (He did.)

"Wy d'yer wear trousers?"

"Want ter see yer 'ouse; funny little 'ouse."

"I'll pinch yer bot agine." (He repeated the performance.)

"Is there birds and wabbits in there wiv yer?" pointing into my hall.

"Come in and see," I invited them.

Hurried protests from the kind lady in attendance.

"Oh, hadn't it better be only two at a time? Their muddy boots! I can't control all those at once."

"Let 'em all come!" I said, but already the invasion had begun, and my little staircase was a river of mixed colours. They flowed into the hall, into my kitchen-dining-room, and, when I managed to get upstairs, on each of my beds I found five gnomes lying abreast, squealing with laughter. Even the bathroom — and the bath itself — overflowed with them. A breathtaking experience which we all thoroughly enjoyed.

In parting, one small perky boy looked up at me with his tousled head on one side and said, "I know yer nime! It's Lady Squirrel." So *much* nicer than Lady Fortescue, and very appropriate to one who persists in living amid woods.

Once a month the mothers of these babies came to visit them, and as the five little lakes, rising one above the other, each connected by a waterfall, lie in this the loveliest part of the estate, the stone steps leading down the rock cliffs from the Big House was always the most popular walk. But always they came in clumps, these mothers, never alone, and from my windows I watched eyes roll wonderingly in the direction of my cottage. One day I talked to one fat matron accompanied by a pretty daughter.

"Oh, me dear, I'm that tired! 'Aven't slept for nights with that Jerry blarstin' us all to bits. Never a night in me own bed and never no sleep in our dug-out. Bombed out twice, we've been, but I've got to stick it 'cos yer see me man's workin' at the docks, and 'e must 'ave 'is supper wen 'e comes in, even if it's in a 'ouse wiv 'arf a roof or dahn in the dug-out. We're not ser bad, are we, Poll?" Then, jerking her thumb at her daughter, "She's 'The Dug-Out Bride' — 'ad 'er picshur in the pipers. 'Er boy come 'ome — ef yer can call it an 'ome now — an' 'e wanted ter get spliced with Poll durin' 'is leave, an' we none of us 'ad no time to get to another church — ours was blitzed — so it wos all done in the dug-out, reception an' all, becos me 'usband couldn't get time off and 'e wanted to be there, so 'e slips off fer 'arf an hour, an' Frank's h'Army chaplain come an' tied 'em up dahn in the dug-out. It's all there, in *The Daily Sketch*, and Poll's 'The Dug-Out Bride' — that there green grass do look so luvverly dahn by that water. Makes yer want ter lie dahn and get some sleep. But if I laid dahn I don't believe I'd ever get up agen — I'm that tired."

"Won't you come and stay the night with me in my cottage?" I begged. "Both of you. On comfortable beds. Grass gets rather damp at night, you know."

"Nah that *is* kind, ma'am, but I must get back to my

ole man an' get 'is supper. Blitz or no Blitz, Jerry shan't do my old man out of 'is ole woman *nor* 'is supper. But — we thanks yer kindly all the sime, don't we, Poll?" Then, rolling an eye towards my cottage, she said: "I do think yer brive, mum, to live dahn 'ere all by yerself. *I* dassent. It'd give me the willies, that it would. Them 'orrid 'ills in the ditime an' the 'ellish 'ush at night. I'd feel a sight sifer in ole London."

Different temperaments: different points of view. That night, alone in my little cottage (quite alone, for I had not yet found Kitty), I put out my lamp and turned on the wireless, hoping for some music before I slept. Immediately the noble strains of Handel's Largo filled my room, and a beautiful contralto voice sang:

"Safe in thy leafy breast
Softly I fall to rest
All cares retreat."

And I smiled to myself, for that was just what I was feeling at that lovely peaceful moment as I looked out into the starlight upon the dim outlines of great protecting trees, smelt the fresh fragrance of moss and dew-wet grass, and heard the sound of many waters.

Yet the mother of "The Dug-Out Bride" felt safer in old London.

CHAPTER
THREE

For My Protection

Autumn passed, a triumphant pageant of colour here in my valley, as though God had mixed all the beautiful blazing heroism of men to-day, all the burning love and prayers of proud and agonized women, all the dazzling dreams and aspirations and high ideals of youth into celestial colours upon a great palette, then painted the trees of the woods, afterwards washing it in the five lakes, staining their cold silver sheen with flaming scarlet and crimson and glimmering gold.

Walking in the woods under this canopy of colour amid breast-high bracken of green and gold, I watched joyous rabbits scudding through the undergrowth, heard the chatter of magpies and the caw of rooks agitated by my passing, noted the vivid emerald of moss cushioned upon great grey rocks. But I was lonely and sad amid this loveliness, thinking of the loneliness and sadness of those I loved in France; missing my little loved Dominie, my Blackness, lonely and sad, too, in his concentration camp. But in December he would be freed from the Quarantine Kennels and our separation of six months ended. "Then you'll have to look to your white bob-tails!" I warned the rabbits. "He's pretty speedy, my Blackness."

As I passed the first lake on my return to the cottage a little moor-hen flew out from the fringing rushes, skimmed over the still surface of the water, then suddenly crash-dived upon it, sending a mass of ripples which, starting with one small silver V, multiplied itself into hundreds of larger and larger V's until the Victory Sign spread from shore to shore. A heartening symbol. Nice little bird.

Across the grass path leading to my door someone had dragged a garden seat from the edge of the lake, setting it where a dreamer could best contemplate the glorious panorama of colour, forgetful of possible broken head or shins of the Lady of the Lake should she return home in darkness. That dreamer could be only one person, the younger son of the Big House now home on leave — musician, poet, artist, writer — and he would certainly never have passed my cottage without coming to see me. There would be a message in the letter-box. But there was only a bunch of late roses from his mother, my White Lady, lying on my doorstep. Nice White Lady: she was known by that name because almost always she dressed in white.

We had made friends, this boy and I, finding instantly that we shared tastes. We had walked together in the woods, and he had found an amphitheatre among the great grey rocks, had sprung upon one of them and declaimed Mark Antony's oration.

"What a setting for a play!" he had cried enthusiastically.

Enchanted with the improvements to my once derelict cottage, he had exacted from me a promise that, at the end of the war, when every one came home again, I would celebrate victory by giving a bonfire picnic down by the lakes. He had tried to help me to cut away undergrowth and overgrowth around the cottage, bringing soldier friends to assist us in our arduous task. It was a hot day, and by luncheon-time my volunteer workers were sticky and exhausted. They knocked off work for a refreshing plunge in the lowest lake before luncheon, promising to return and "finish off and clear up" afterwards.

"I shall never see you again. You'll eat an enormous luncheon and then lie like gorged snakes in the sun and sleep it off," was my final taunt as they disappeared up the rock steps of the cliff. I was perfectly right. I saw no more of them. The poor Lady of the Lake had to clear up the mess they had made in her valley, bless them!

Some time after his departure I received a most exciting-looking parcel addressed in an unknown hand. I was drinking my morning coffee in bed when this was brought in to me, and, as my absurd way is with surprise parcels, I put off opening it just to tantalise myself, so that my inner excitement quietly grew as I opened and read my letters, skimmed the newspaper, and smoked a cigarette, with the ash-tray perched on the precious parcel which I placed on my tumpkin.

At last I could bear it no more, so, having no knife or scissors near me, and being too cozy to get out of bed to find some, I burned the confining string of my parcel with my cigarette end till it broke. Then I unwrapped the contents — two beautiful antique pistols — and

A TIN OF GUNPOWDER ——! On a slip of paper was scrawled:

"For your safety. One to protect each end of your valley. I wish I had time to give these weapons a worthier sheen."

What a splendid base for an ash-tray holding a burning cigarette — a tin of gunpowder. . . . "For your safety." . . . And then HOW I laughed! Oh, how I laughed and LAUGHED. Only a poet and a dreamer could have sent me so romantic a gift, and I knew at once the identity of the donor.

Late that night I tiptoed forth with a torch and gingerly peppered one of the lakes with the gunpowder lest it aid the conflagration of a stray incendiary bomb should one inadvertently fall upon my cottage. Only a sleepy swan witnessed this stealthy deed.

It was not until very long afterwards that I learned from the elder brother, my landlord — who, instead of being amused by my story, was both shocked and irate — that the gunpowder sent was only dud gunpowder and non-explosive. This information was elicited from the strafed donor by the horrified warning of the elder brother: "You *can't* do things like that. You know it's illegal to send gunpowder by post. And don't you realise that SHE MIGHT PUT YOU INTO ONE OF HER BOOKS!"

Well, I have! Forgive me, dear boy, if you ever read this, but I simply couldn't resist it. James, the swan, didn't die of a surfeit of gunpowder, and you shall have your bonfire picnic when you come home again. I think you deserve it. In the meantime your beautiful pistols may not serve as a protection for the Lady of the Lake, but at least they make her laugh whenever she looks at them, and, after all, laughter is the greatest weapon we have.

I laughed again when the Rector of our village, who, I had heard, was a Canon or some big gun of the Church, paid me his first call. He arrived carrying a most handsome broccoli, which he presented to me with a courtly bow.

"So far from civilisation, I thought that this might come in useful," he said, with a twinkle.

It was the first time I'd ever been "bunched" with broccoli, but I suppose when one has reached the fifties one can expect nothing else. And it was quite delicious served *au gratin*.

I asked the Canon a further favour. Would he perhaps come one day and bless my little home. In Provence my two homes had each been blessed in turn — by two dear Bishops. I felt that I should settle down more cosily in my cottage when it had been blessed.

He gave ready assent, and some days later came with his wife, a great lover of France, who vested him in cassock, snow-white surplice and stole for the little ceremony, which the dear, learned old man performed with great dignity and simplicity. But, oddly enough, though he had so thoughtfully catered for its needs on his first visit, he forgot to bless my kitchen!

CHAPTER
FOUR

James

November — and the rain. I suppose only a millionaire who can afford to chase the sun outside Europe can like the month of November, a month of sludgy mud, dank dead leaves, fog, and a smell of wet decay. Even in Provence we dreaded November, the month of torrential rains which often washed down the supporting walls of our terraces, when the blessed sun was hidden and skies were grey — everything was grey, because a land of silvery olive trees and grey rocks looks greyer than anywhere in England could ever look, even in November.

Down in my valley it couldn't have been wetter, but the grass was still green and the blood-red bark of dogwood and the orange of osiers supplied touches of colour around the leaden lakes, which brimmed and then over-brimmed their borders. Kind people feared that the Lady of the Lake might one day be washed out of her cottage — all save her landlord, who pointed out to her that she could always climb up on to the great rock outside the house should floods surround it. That rock had a history. Legend had it that the miller who once inhabited the old mill cottage, replaced by the solid quaint little Redness which now stands on the old site, was rather a villain, with a sense of humour. Though deeply in debt to all in the neighbourhood he still frequented its houses of call, where he ran up more bills for beer. The landlord of one public-house at last grew impatient of promises to pay, and demanded something more solid in return for a glass of beer. Whereupon the miller suggested that the man should accept in payment a beautiful horse-trough which could be found outside the mill cottage. So the landlord gave him beer, and then more beer, and the next day descended the precipice to take away his horse-trough. The miller (I am sure with a grin) led him to the great rock outside the cottage in which was hewn the trough, and begged him to take it away if he liked.

There was no sign of the trough when I took the cottage, for the top of the rock was overgrown with nettles, but since it had been suggested to me as a rock of refuge should the flooded lakes attempt to overwhelm me, I thought it might be well to exterminate the nettles. So putting on heavy gardening gauntlets, I climbed the rock to clean its top. Those who have uprooted nettles will know how the roots run and layer and mat together if left to grow for a long time. As I dragged up a bunch I was fascinated to find that a complete mat of nettles rose up as I pulled. The shallow soil which had blown and sifted on to the rock during the course of years failed to give the roots of my nettles resistance, and triumphantly I saw the swift end of what I had feared would be a long job. Underthe matted roots was clean bare rock — *and* the miller's trough! There it unmistakably was — a deep oblong trough cut into

25

the stone — and beside it was scratched deeply a rough shield with initials carved within it — P.J.H. and a half-effaced date which began with 18 —. Rough steps led up to it. After this discovery I ceased not to enquire of every ancient inhabitant of our village and neighbouring villages to find out if anyone still living could remember the name of that legendary miller, and at last I discovered a very old man who began to chuckle before I had finished my description. *That*, he mumbled, was one of his great-grandfather's best stories, that one about old Miller Holland. HOLLAND! P.J.H.! Almost that old miller took flesh and blood and bones before me. Almost I could see the twinkle in his eyes and hear his wicked laugh.

Only James the Swan seemed to enjoy the November rains. He was nearly as legendary a person as Holland, though he still haunted the valley in feathered form — a lovely graceful form when sailing majestically around the lakes, but ridiculous and ungainly when waddling with great flat turned-in feet to my cottage door. Perhaps it was loneliness — or was it greed? — that made him so persistent a nuisance, for nuisance he was, hissing ferociously and flapping great wings if not given bread, so that every one feared to pass him without propitiatory crusts in the pocket. Only they never seemed to be in the pocket, and my mule-bell was for ever ringing to summon my aid — in the form of bread. My baker's bill was doubled because of James, and in the end, to save myself endless journeys to the kitchen, I filled my letter-box with crusts for callers. I tried hard to be sorry for James because of his solitary state. His wife had died, and, when a second wife was given him for consolation, he just killed her. Then he became morose and, as I learned later, sometimes murderous. But I found him a Bore with a capital B. Still, he had character, had James, and in the end I firmly believed the story that once he had been found sitting in an armchair by the fire in one of the lodge-keepers' kitchens. He was always trying to come into mine, and no discourtesy on my part seemed to discourage him, though on the whole he was fairly polite, in a sullen way, to me, so that I wasn't afraid of him, although I distrusted him deeply.

James was an elusive swan, and one never knew upon which lake or path in the woods one would find him. He travelled for miles on those flat feet, often climbing the precipice and waddling along the main road until lost to sight. He would be absent for a day or two and then suddenly a gleam of white would be seen on his favourite lake — and there was James, back again. Once he visited a soldiers' camp, and the C.O. telephoned to inform my landlord that his swan was sharing a meal with them in the mess. A gardener was sent over to herd James home. A gregarious swan, it would seem; perhaps one of those males who are at their best with other males, yet bully women. Certainly James bullied me, and I am not the type that rather enjoys being bullied. Also I have a raging sense of equity, and if I give bread — unlimited bread — when I secretly long to give a stone, I expect at least a glimmer of gratitude from the recipient. But did I get it? The answer is NO. All I got was a black bruised thigh when passing James during the (unsuspected by me) mating season. My propitiatory crust ignored, a terrifying hiss, a snake-like neck suddenly uncoiled, a great yellow beak stabbing for my eye and two vast pinions flapping at my flying form, the tip of one of them just catching me with violence between hip and knee as I scrambled up a bank under the shelter of low-spreading branches whither James could not quickly or easily follow. Breakfast on the mantelpiece for days, and I became a Black-leg.

I warned the inmates of the Big House that James had become dangerous for a season, lest he attack those London babies during their innocent walks abroad, for one of the great events of their day was to feed the swan.

"Where's Jimes? *Dear* Jimes!"

Dear Jimes indeed!

Thenceforth and for some time I was forced to make surreptitious sorties from my cottage, for James now apparently hated me and seemed to enjoy terrorising me and keeping me captive. Before going out I peered cautiously from my windows, and if James was sitting on my front doorstep, then I stole out by the kitchen door and made a wide detour into the woods where, believe it or not it is true, I might easily find James sailing around the farthest lake, having reached it with most uncanny speed, and on sight of me, thrashing his way across it like a destroyer (the swift naval kind) to ruin my walk if possible. A bully.

Now that we are on the subject of James I will prematurely record his end. While he was dangerous my landlord kindly caused to be erected a barricade of wire-netting across the inlet under a little bridge through which James sailed when he desired to leave his favourite lake far away in the woods to come to mine to bully me. This barrier was placed, naturally, when James was absent, and with what relief did I see my little lakes empty of swan! For a time there was peace. I was thankful for this, because my friends, braving the precipice in all weathers to come and visit me, turned and fled when they saw James keeping guard on my doorstep. One friend had had her arm broken by the pinions of a swan, and had a wholesome distrust of the breed ever after.

So that I was thankful for that barricade, and then, this very November, floods washed it away, and once again I was haunted by James. I implored one of the gardeners to wait until the swan had gone to the lake in the woods and then work overtime to replace that barrier. I promised him a handsome reward if he would do this, and before he started the work myself verified his statement that James was indeed on the lake in the deeper woods, so that he was not shut in for ever with me. The barrier was well and truly made, and the gardener laboured long and arduously in its making, becoming soaked with water and mud. He deserved and got his reward.

Next day, walking warily in the woods, I could see no trace of James, nor for days afterwards, although I expected to meet him at every turning of every path. No one worried about his absence because of his known partiality for wandering off and visiting strange places. He had vanished before, but always he had come back.

This time he did not come back, and one day a heap

of blood-stained feathers that once had clothed James like white samite, mystic, wonderful, was found amid the bracken. A fox had surprised him in his sleep. Even by his death, just when I had secured myself from his presence in so costly a manner, James had the laugh of me.

CHAPTER
FIVE

The Blackness is Liberated

December dawned, and I grew more and more excited, for in a few days my Blackness would be released from the Quarantine Kennels, and I could hardly wait to see the joy of liberation. After six months of solitary confinement I could imagine how heavenly freedom would seem. Already I could see him rioting in these lovely woods, chasing those daring rabbits, perhaps putting up a stray pheasant, new delights for a dog born and bred in the South of France where game is seldom seen, even in the mountains. The fact that the woods on this private estate were not preserved had finally decided me to lease "Many Waters." It would be so lovely for my Dominie to learn the thrill of hunting. And I wanted to make a home quickly for my beloved *Mademoiselle* and our other dear neighbour in Provence should they find conditions out there intolerable and escape to England. I knew that if they did come they would arrive quite destitute, and for weeks I had been knitting soft white woollies in which to wrap *Mademoiselle*, who always got ill in cold damp weather. I feared our English climate for her. I had also filled in a landing licence for little Squibs, her shadow dog, who would assuredly accompany her if she came, for I remembered how I had suffered myself, at St. Malo, when I discovered that without a landing licence (which had been early applied for but lost in the turmoil of war) my Blackness was not allowed to set paw in England. I have described that agony in another book,* and have been criticised by certain readers for what they considered over-emphasis on the fate of a dog at a tragic moment like that of Dunkirk, when the lives of so many thousands hung in the balance. But, as Dominie's Quarantine Kennels proved, those same men whose lives were in jeopardy at Dunkirk shared my views on dogs. The majority of the dogs in these kennels were refugee dogs. Fleeing from the land which had for them become a hell of fire and mad terror they rushed into the sea and swam after the "little ships". What British soldier in the world would let a dog drown even to save himself? Those poor terrified animals were hauled into already over-crowded boats, sheltered, comforted, and finally housed in the Quarantine Kennels. When I visited Dominie I sometimes had the felicity of witnessing the reunion of an anxious searching officer with his dog, which had been lost at that awful moment. An hysterical yelp of recognition, followed by every joyful canine sound and song, a barred door opened and a khaki figure down on his knees in the cell, caressing a leaping, licking mass of ecstasy. I would quickly avert my eyes from what should be a secret sacred thing, but my heart sang for joy.

*Trampled Lilies, Wm. Blackwood & Sons, Ltd.

Although lectured by some, I have had many more letters from people with loved dogs of their own, telling me that as they read of my Dominie they were thankful that I was able, after all, to bring him to England in safety. My Blackness has now a "fan mail" of his own, and last Christmas received seven personal parcels containing his favourite charcoal biscuits, luscious horse-meat, a collar, a lead, a ball, besides calendars and cards; and two strange ladies travelled all the way from Eastbourne, braving the precipice, just for a glimpse of him.

Well, I had taken "Many Waters" for the shelter and happiness of these Beloveds of mine, and soon should have the black one under my roof. I had visited him in his camp almost every week, taking with me a little tin pot full of the delicacies he loved, and we always lunched together in his run, and I spent the day with him, combing him and brushing him and having mad games. The kennel man could never quite forgive him because he had failed to win my Blackness's heart, whereas he was adored by every other dog in the kennels. Dominie, always a nervous person, distrusted men ever since the French Army marched into our village at the moment of *Mobilisation Générale* and overran my house, occupying all the corners hitherto sacred to him. He hated loud male voices and the thud of heavy boots from that moment, and the kennel man — a great dear and a great character — possessed both. Dominie much preferred the proprietor of the kennels, a wounded ex-officer of the last war, who happily possessed a deep voice and gentle ingratiating fingers which knew where to tickle.

"'E's a little snob-dawg, yours is, your ladyship," the

kennel man complained to me. "'E won't let me come near 'im, but when the boss appears on the scene 'e's all waggles. I shall 'ave ter learn ter talk like the snobs — *Dermenee! Dermeenee! Good* little dawg! Hew air yew this morning, my little fellah?"

But from even that address my Blackness shrank, rolling apprehensive eyes at me.

Well ——! It would soon be over now, and another ache overpast.

I could console myself a little bit with the dogs of my neighbours. My landlord possessed an enormous imperial red setter, a magnificent beast who loped up and down the rock cliffs with powerful untiring stride, leaping every seemingly impossible fence and obstacle that came in his way. I had seen him lying on the terrace of the Big House when I first called for the keys to inspect my jackdaws' cottage, and I had asked the White Lady whether her dog was good with other dogs because I possessed one, much beloved, the only thing of any value to me (except my mother's miniature) rescued from France. She replied that her noble-looking Romulus enjoyed little dogs, and seeing him running among those London babies, who all seemed to love him, I was reassured about his gentleness. After my installation he often came down with my landlord to visit me, and sat with a huge paw on my knee.

"The three girls" of my log supplier, adorable little cairns, were another consolation when I climbed up to their rambling old house on the other side of the valley to visit him and his queenly wife. She had a splendid brain and an understanding heart, and the gay gallantry with which she faced the war problems which beset us all won my instant sympathy and admiration. I liked the atmosphere of that happy old house lined with well-worn, well-loved books: I enjoyed sitting in the deep chintz-covered armchairs and smelling the atmosphere of wood-smoke, flowers and tobacco as I drank my tea, while the grandmother cairn (first generation) sat, as always, in her own *chaise-longue* near her adored master, the granddaughter cairn (third generation) upon his knee — and sometimes upon mine if she decided so to honour me — while the daughter cairn sat near her mistress.

Returning through the woods from one of those happy tea-parties, on a night of sparkling, exhilarating frost and starlight, I so far forgot my grey curls and advancing years as to *dance* down the paths, waving my electric torch in rhythm with the little tune I was humming. Everything looked so lovely and silvery, and the air smelled of chrysanthemums (have you ever noticed that frost smells like chrysanthemums?), there were silver cobwebs stretching across the narrow paths, silver dust was sprinkled on the glossy leaves of rhododendrons, coarse grass had been transformed into tiny silver spears, silver stars glittered above me, and some had fallen into the lakes and glittered still. Every time my dancing feet touched the ground there was a crisp little ghostly scrunch of frost. I think the burden of my song was, "The Blackness will soon be here!" or something equally ridiculous, but a frosty atmosphere can even go to a frosted head, and, after all, there was nobody to witness this innocent if undignified performance.

So do we deceive ourselves.

I reached my cottage, and had hardly let myself in and pulled off my mountain shoes in the hall when I was startled by a loud knock upon the door behind me. Opening it, I saw the butler from the Big House, another friend of mine.

"Excuse me, your ladyship, but did anyone come past here? Up at the Big House they saw signalling going on in the woods, a torch flashing up and down and all over the place. They were afraid something funny might be going on — parachutists or something — and you and Kitty alone down here."

Oh heavens! MY TORCH! "There is nothing hidden that shall not be revealed," as the Bible says. Even my innocent, lighthearted, undignified little dance must be observed from the Big House.

"*I* came in a minute ago, Hatherway," I said, and then, always recognising a kindred spirit when I see one, I decided to confess!

"I fear that it was I, dancing through the woods, Hatherway. It's such a lovely night that one had to do something about it — I forgot my torch might be seen — in fact, I forgot everything except the loveliness."

"Certainly, your ladyship." Hatherway's mouth wavered for a second into his characteristic crooked smile, but it was full of sympathy.

"Was I waving my torch about much, Hatherway?" I enquired anxiously.

"Well — you were — *a bit*, your ladyship," he replied, with a gleam in his blue eyes and the ghost of a deprecatory smile.

"Yes, I fear I was," I admitted, remembering the windmill gestures of the arms which had accompanied leaping trousered legs. Then, dismissing the incident, I said:

"Won't you come in and let me show you my cottage? You've never seen it since it was furnished."

Shouts from the cliffs suddenly rent the starlit night.

"They're thinking I've been done in by parachutists. I must go back, your ladyship, thank you very much. Since you and Kitty are all right — good night, your ladyship."

"Good night, Hatherway — and thank you so much for coming down."

So that was that, and I was left wondering if that incorrigible child which makes up so large a part of me would ever grow up and learn to behave like a sedate matron. The worst of it is that real children instantly recognise the *gamine* in me and become delightfully demoralised in my company. Even that London slum baby knew that he could pinch my bot with impunity and only risk a laugh or, at most, a sly return pinch on his. Well, as my man would have said, "There the matter is."

Kitty had been much amused by my early and ceaseless preparations for the coming home of The Blackness. My first purchase when buying furniture had been a huge basket of plaited rushes and a green blanket and cushion for Dominie's bed, and this had lain empty by my bedside ever since, unless his etheric body had been curled up where his spirit surely always was. When buying that basket I really knew that it would prove a cumbrous obstacle in my room and entirely superfluous, because since his first night spent with me in France as a tiny puppy, when no less than thirty times he crawled on to my pillow out of a superb new basket prepared for him, until at length (as he very well knew I should be) I was too weary to repeat the performance of putting him back into it, he has obstinately persisted in sleeping on my bed. Still, the buying and furnishing of the rush basket was at least a gesture to show him when he came that it was HIS cottage — that I had been impatiently awaiting his arrival. To assure him of this there were drinking bowls placed on the floor of every room, a special tin of charcoal biscuits, a set of green towels to dry filthy feathered feet after walks in the woods; a supply of horse-meat was assured, and a special board and knife purchased; there was a hard rubber ball which (I hoped) could not be instantly destroyed, and other little items of no interest to the reader, but of deep interest to him.

On the wonderful Day of Liberation it had been arranged that I should spend the week-end with my brother and his family in Hertfordshire, collecting The Blackness *en route*. He would be so happy running about the huge garden and surrounding fields with two golden cocker girls, and a staid little cairn as chaperon. So I got into my cockle-shell and drove off, complete with a brand-new dog-collar and lead (gift of the household I was now to visit), a prepared luncheon in a bowl and a few charcoal biscuits in my pocket.

So eager and early was my arrival at the kennels that the two poor overworked kennel men, who now had one hundred and fifty refugee dogs to care for, besides cats, and the pigs and poultry of the boss, had not yet had time to give Dominie his outgoing bath and grooming. His own especial kennel man apologised for this, and asked me if I would care to wait while this was done, but I had walked straight into Dominie's run, and, when the frantic fervour of his greeting was abated, had already put on his collar and attached his lead. As though he understood the suggestion of his kennel man, The Blackness picked up the end of the dragging lead in his mouth, looked imploringly at me and waltzed to the door of his run still holding it, then looked back, his eyes plainly saying: "We've had enough of this. Come ON! Let's GET OUT!"

So, dusty but deliriously happy, did Dominie leave that kind concentration camp, and equally dusty from the battering of joyous paws, and equally happy because at last this hideous separation was ended, did I lead him, dancing and singing in a most unmelodious and hysterical canine voice, to my car. Together we drove away, though our progress was slow because, for some long time, I was obliged to stop the engine so that once again we might embrace.

Our week-end was a success. I could never tire of watching those four feathered liberated legs tearing over the smooth green lawns of my brother's rectory garden (soon to grow shaggy and shabby as did we humans. But then it was *chic* to be shabby, wasn't it?) It was such joy to witness the marathon races of Dominie with Treacle and Duchy, the two golden girls, and little Tess, the chaperon-cairn, trotting far behind, yapping admonitions and barking her sharp disapproval

39

when the three breathless forms plunged into the little river which flows through the grounds. My four nieces, shouting encouragement, tore after the dogs, and all was noisy happiness.

Our drive back to Sussex was happy too, especially the proud moment when, letting Dominie out into a field for a run, he put up his first pheasant in truly professional cocker style. When we reached the top of my precipice he showed by every means in his power that he was thrilled with the woods and rocks, and I had some difficulty in keeping him to the right-of-way when so many fascinating distant scents allured him. I promised him a riot in the woods on the morrow, but unkindly Fate forced me to break my word. Inside the cottage he tore up and down the stairs, visiting every room in turn, immediately made hay of his bedding in the beautiful new basket with a few disdainful kicks, then leaped up at my bed and almost winked at me.

"I thought you'd say that," I answered him.

Time for supper — and I prepared such a lovely one for him of fresh luscious horse-meat and biscuit which, to my consternation, he seemed to have some difficulty in swallowing. He was obviously ravenously hungry, but to swallow seemed painful, and then he began to make queer choking sounds and to slaver. Horrified, I took him into a good light, opened his mouth, peered down his throat, and there, wedged across it, was a wicked-looking rabbit bone. When and where had he picked up this dangerous and forbidden thing? How I longed for *Mademoiselle*! Once in the High Alps this same thing had happened — a rabbit bone filched from somewhere and pouched, unsuspected by us, until such a time as it could be devoured surreptitiously. We had both agonised with him, but *Mademoiselle* had dealt with the matter in her own masterly and experienced way. Now I must deal with this alone, for Kitty had no experience with dogs.

I tried to reach the bone, but Dominie struggled at the critical moment and jogged my arm, so that all I succeeded in doing was to push it farther down. We spent an awful night, my poor little man swimming about on the floor, rubbing his poor throat along the carpet, scratching at it desperately, jumping up on to my bed and imploring me to do something about it. We tried raw white of egg, we tried hard crusts, but nothing could relieve him. As soon as it was light I must drive to a friend six miles away and get from her the address of the vet she had so strongly recommended to me some weeks ago.

In the grey light of a winter morning The Blackness, a very chastened little Blackness led by a very weary mother, reascended the precipice and got out the car. Gallant little thing, she started with one turn of the handle and climbed easily over the rocky ground, a gradient of one in three.

Arrived at my friend's house, we were shown up into her bedroom, and then I learned that the vet lived another five miles farther on! She kindly began to describe the un-signposted route to me, but evidently realising that in my dazed and weary condition I should probably never find my way, she suddenly said:

"My brother is an early riser, and I believe he

would enjoy the drive with you if you can bring him back here."

I babbled my gratitude, and presently her elderly brother appeared and consented to show me the way, though when he saw my tiny car and the poor dribbling little Dominie seated in the armchair-seat next the driver's, he looked doubtful.

"Could your dog sit at the back?" he asked. "I don't know whether my long legs would curl up into so confined a space."

"We'll try him," I said, then added apologetically, "but I'm afraid he may be difficult. You see, that has always been his place since he was a puppy, driving alone with me in France."

We effected the change of place, heaving Dominie's rug and my handbag on to the back seat, and finally cajoling him to jump into it too. Then my guide wound up his long legs and got in beside me. Hardly had I started the engine than the offended Blackness climbed up on my shoulders and from thence struggled down upon the wheel, from which he fiercely refused to be displaced.

"If your dog's going to do that, I think I'd rather be cramped than killed," remarked my guide grimly. And so, once again, I stopped the engine and opened the door, feeling in my bones that the kind man was already thinking "D— this d— woman and her d— dog!"

Those possessing or having possessed a Baby Austin of ancient type will remember the inconvenience of only one door a side, so that to allow anyone to reach or escape from the back seat the person seated in front of him must first get out and tilt up his armchair to provide egress for the escapist. This generally entails a cascade of rugs and other impedimenta — generally gloves and maps — into the road.

The transference completed we drove on, the driver feeling somewhat hot and ashamed of all the pother her poor little animal was causing.

Arrived at the vet the little animal was carefully examined with reflecting mirror fixed to forehead, electric lamp and so on. There was no sign of the bone. He had swallowed it.

Luckily I can laugh in moments like these. And I did. There was still the danger of perforation by that mischievous bone, and I was given powders to administer hourly to dissolve it. If haemorrhage set in —

I ceased to laugh.

And I was very near tears when on looking for my bag to pay the vet his fee I found it not. We must have tipped it into the road during that exchange of seats. Or I might have left it in my friend's house? It was *not* in her house, and neither notices of its loss posted in the shops of the neighbouring town with the offer of a handsome reward, nor the conscience of its finder, who could read my name and address on identity card, ration book and the envelopes of several letters addressed to me, ever brought it back. You see, Mummie's miniature set in gold, a large lump of turquoise matrix also set in gold, all my petrol coupons and various personal treasures — beside my cheque book and a bundle of notes — were of even greater value to that thief. But when he had prised off the golden frame, he might have returned me Mummie's miniature backed by her lovely hair, for that could have no value for him, whereas to me its price was far above rubies.

And so that joyful time of home-coming was marred.

CHAPTER
SIX

Romulus and Rema

The next morning some duty or another took me up the precipice at noon, the hour sacred to the dinner of Dominie. I had instructed Kitty in its careful preparation, warning her that for a day or two we must go very gently, however ravenous he appeared to be. She pleaded to be allowed to feed him, feeling (rightly) sure that this would be the surest and quickest way of gaining his confidence. She had fallen an immediate victim to his charm, and her work had been seriously delayed by flirtatious flicks with a duster as she passed him. A gleam in his eye and his head tilted to one side as he watched her showed me that he found these overtures both pleasing and promising; they might lead to riotous games later on. Margharita's yellow dusters had proved an endless source of joy in France, and one and all bore traces of Dominie's teeth. In fact, Margharita had ruined for ever his inborn talent for retrieving, so carefully fostered and trained by me, because she never coaxed him to return her duster when he fetched it from a chair, but rather ran after him laughing and protesting until the pursuit ended in a mad chase all over the house and garden, if not a disastrous (to the duster) tug-of-war. Dominie must have missed those splendid games with his slave Margharita while he sat lonely in his hut at the Quarantine Kennels, and now was looking hopefully at the quickly subjugated Kitty, who might perhaps, if subtly fascinated by alluring attitudes — flicker of what was supposed to be a tail and tiny muffled growls — develop into quite a good playmate too. So I left them together and went out.

Half-way up the precipice I heard the loud chatter of many babies approaching, and round a bend trotted a crowd of gnomes and elves surrounding a slender, excitable red setter bitch.

"It's Rema! Rema's come back agine! We loves Rema!"

Who was Rema? Their L.C.C. instructor informed me that Rema had once belonged to the Big House, but had been given to a lady who had now returned her because she found Rema inconvenient in war-time. What a moment to choose!

WHAT a bore! The presence of a lady dog would now create jealousy between the males, and if it came to a fight between rivals, the bitch would surely join in with that majestic powerful old gentleman with whom I had made friends. Dominie being a Free Frenchman would certainly be both free and French when he met this charming lady. He adores the other sex and simply *must* philander.

My heart misgave me, and when I met my White Lady I confided my misgivings to her. We decided that the dogs must meet on neutral ground — not anywhere near my cottage, which my little black man would now consider his duty to protect against all comers — and my White Lady assured me that she could control her big Romulus if he showed signs of jealousy.

The dreaded meeting was to take place on the morrow near the lowest lake (in case of the necessity for forced immersion). My White Lady would stroll past with her dogs, and I was asked to wait until she disappeared from sight before I came out with Dominie. She said Romulus would be perfectly good if with her. When the moment came I own that I felt physically sick, for nothing in the world unnerves me like a dog fight, and, if it came to this, the odds would be so terribly against my poor little man, who would be overwhelmed in a two-to-one encounter. So I begged a friend who was staying with me to come too, armed — as I was — with a stick and a pepper-pot, and when the White Lady had vanished with her two red terrors around a clump of rhododendrons, we started. But we had timed our start a few minutes too late, and when we reached the clearing in the woods which we had selected as a meeting place, so that there was a chance that all the dogs would then start off on a friendly rabbit hunt, we found it empty; the White Lady had strolled on. We followed her tracks along a narrow path bordering the lake, and then suddenly the worst possible thing happened. She made a sudden appearance, muffled up in a heavy fur coat, from a dark tunnel cut in the rhododendrons. Now the nervous Dominie, born in the hot sunshine of the Midi, had never before seen a human being inside a fur coat, and I honestly think that he imagined its wearer to be some large animal which might be ferocious, and was certainly too big for him to tackle. He checked, his hackles went up, and he gave a low growl, warning the animal that at any rate it had better not touch *me*. His trouble is that he always imagines that everybody, human or canine, has designs upon my life, and I find this excessively protective attitude extremely trying and quite superfluous. Hearing this defensive growl, the two red terrors hastened to the scene to protect *their* mistress, and then Dominie made his second *faux pas*. Seeing before him a beautiful red-haired girl, he became one seductive waggle and pranced joyously up to Rema. The red-haired maiden, quick and uncertain of temper as are many of her lovely colouring, snapped at him, and then the red male advanced upon The Blackness with slow, purposeful steps, bristling, with intent to kill! The White Lady called him commandingly to her side, but Romulus ignored her and still came on. It was then that my friend could bear no more.

"Turn slowly round and walk away, then call Dominie," she hissed in my ear.

I, too, had had enough. I obeyed orders, and, thank God, after a few offensive growls, The Blackness did follow me. We had so lately been reunited that perhaps he thought it better not to let me out of his sight again. The White Lady hurried off in the opposite direction, diverting the attention of her dogs to rabbit-holes. But the jealous feud was started. That night I seemed to see the flaming sword which I had prayed might never bar the gates of my Paradise. Henceforth, whenever Dominie and I wandered in it, I should be in terror of his life. One big dog I might have tackled — but two!

When my landlord came home for the week-end

he descended the cliff to visit me and to make the acquaintance of Dominie. When I told him of the unfortunate meeting of the dogs he looked worried.

"I don't know why it is, but Romulus has always hated cocker spaniels, especially black ones," he confided to me unhappily.

A silence of consternation. Then:

"Perhaps if you bring him down one day, on a strong lead, and I put Dominie on a lead, and we take them for a walk together, they might get used to each other?" I suggested, rather doubtfully.

"We might try it to-morrow," he agreed, in an equally doubtful tone.

Try it we did, and never was failure more complete. His red dog fought and strained to get at Dominie, whose behaviour on that occasion was irreproachable, though the aspect of his enemy was truly terrifying — bared fangs, slavering mouth, eyes that glared so madly that their whites were visible around the iris. After a few moments of struggle and command my landlord — a big strong man, shouted: "Take your dog indoors quickly. I can't control mine any more. He's trying to turn on me."

So I fled precipitately towards the cottage, towing with me a bewildered Blackness, and once inside I sat heavily down in a chair because my legs would no longer support me.

A pitiful admission of cowardice, but I would far rather brave the hairpin bends of the High Alps in a car (and they TERRIFIED me) than be mixed up in a dog-fight when primitive passions are unloosed and

49

only brute force (of which I possess none) can separate the combatants.

"Hold your dog up by his tail," advised someone long ago.

"But he hasn't GOT one!" I wailed in despair. And when, months later, my counsellor first saw the little round black bot of The Blackness, exactly like the stern of a bear, with its tiny blob of a flickering tail, docked in the French fashion, our eyes met in reminiscence — and the rest was laughter.

After that ineffective effort to reconcile our dogs, my landlord realised the hopelessness of it. He could only suggest that when his animals came in to be fed at one o'clock every day, they should afterwards be tied to the table legs until half-past two, so that Dominie and I might roam the woods in safety. My thanks were, I fear, a trifle hollow for two reasons — one was the immediately foreseen difficulty for Kitty, who had the complete cottage to clean (and it is a double cottage) and fires to light. Henceforth, if The Blackness was to have any exercise at all, Kitty must now prepare luncheon for me to be ready soon after twelve. How would the poor child receive this suggestion? My second misgiving was this. If those red terrors were rabbiting and ranging the woods two miles away at quarter to one, when Hatherway was called up (and he had already had his Army papers), who would go and search for them, capture these wild collarless animals, take them home and tie them up? My landlord had to be in London every day. There remained his mother and the cook, the former occupied by the babies in the Big House and her music, and the latter with culinary duties. The answer to that question was — NO ONE. Well, the earliest Paradise we know of was infested with a snake, and mine was to be infested with red setters.

My first misgiving proved groundless. My gallant little Kitty accepted the new hour for luncheon as though she were a Provençale — there remained THE SECOND.

CHAPTER
SEVEN

Evacuees

In Provence it is the custom to plant two cypresses at one's gate, one for Peace and the other for Prosperity. I noticed that the Peace cypress was always much smaller than the other, and in some cases had died, leaving only one dark sentinel on guard. When I remarked on this strange fact to an old peasant, he gave me a quick look and a toothless grin as he reminded me that this was quite natural, for, although many people were prosperous in this world, very few knew real peace.

How true. Now here was I, living in the centre of the Circles of Peace, and yet my mind and heart could never rest — because of France. Had I planted two cypresses, one each side of my cottage door on the day of entry, the one on the left (Peace) would have already begun to wilt. There was the constant haunting fear for the health and safety of *Mademoiselle*, and I could get no word of love and comfort to her, nor receive any news of her welfare. My letters to her were returned to me by the British censor, marked "Service Suspended." We were completely cut off from each other, and our work for France had ended tragically. For me there was some hope of its renewal, in some manner, here in England. Already I had acted as interpreter in various hospitals where wounded Frenchmen from Dunkirk were placed at first. Since then they had all been concentrated into one large hospital run by the French, where all the doctors, nurses and helpers were French or spoke French, so that I was no longer needed in that capacity. When I visited the headquarters of General de Gaulle to offer my services, I was received by his Chief of Staff, who was sitting at a desk piled high with papers. To my delight he told me that that mass of correspondence before him consisted chiefly of letters from lovers of France, like myself all eager and willing to offer help in her hour of need. I spoke of *Mademoiselle*'s organisation of FOYERS DES SOLDATS DE FRANCE, and of our work with and for the French Army since the moment of *Mobilisation Générale*. He had heard of it, glanced at my credentials and my proud *laissez-passer* for the army zones, signed by a great lover of England, the ex-Governor of Corsica and then of Briançon; he gave me a beautiful French bow, and told me that when they had co-ordinated and categorised all these generous offers of help from their English allies, I should be approached, and begged to become an honoured member of any association that might be formed. But at present everything was *en l'air*, he said, running his fingers through his hair until that, too, was in the air.

So here in my cottage I must wait with what patience I could summon until once again I was needed to work for France. But, for *Mademoiselle*, all was finished. She was confined within her property, spied upon by the Gestapo, and I knew how that burning spirit of hers must consume her. Our other dear neighbour from Opio had escaped before the armistice with Germany. It was signed while she was being tossed by a violent storm in a tiny yacht (pronounced unseaworthy before starting with its amateur crew of escaping English) outside Oran. By a miracle she eventually reached England, where after a short rest she, with the utmost gallantry, went to work in a huge munition factory, rising at dawn and trudging two miles to her work (later through snow), working full time too, though she is some years older than I and has a worse disability than mine.

Months later we were informed by the authorities that communication, by cable, had been re-established with Unoccupied France, and thenceforward scarcely a week passed without my sending a reply-paid cable to *Mademoiselle*. These messages, she told me in her replies, were precious links to her and made time seem less long. No one will ever know the joy I had when I read her first reply after that deathly silence.

My happiest hours at that time were those I spent with Dominie in the woods, for although they were fraught with anxiety, and always my eyes and ears strained for sounds of red Romulus no one could have remained unaffected by the wild ecstasy of my freed Blackness. He raced ahead of me, leaping through the russet bracken when it impeded his headlong speed. Sometimes I saw at intervals only a laughing face and two black banners of ears suddenly appearing above the golden fern, vanishing and reappearing as he jumped obstacles hidden in the undergrowth. Then he would vanish for a time, and I strove to keep calm, praying silently that those red terrors would not roar down upon him wherever he was and savage him before I could reach that unknown but surely distant spot. And then I would hear a familiar voice far above me on the rock cliffs, and looking up would see the face of my Blackness laughing down at me. I had imagined him to be far below me in the valley. Once he put up a hare. Surely the greatest moment of his life. The chase was almost ludicrous to the onlooker, for that enormous hare seemed larger than its small black pursuer. They vanished through a gully, between great rocks leading to an upper level, Dominie screaming with excitement. I panted after them, wondering where that hare would lead him and knowing that the precious hour and a half of safe liberty was nearing its end. Scrambling over the rocks, ploughing through dead leaves, I reached the plateau — and there stood spell-bound. Fifty yards away from me the hare had checked and was sitting up on its hind legs, immobile as a statue carved in wood. Two yards away from it sat The Blackness — staring at the scenery but NOT at that dreadful beast which was defying all normal customs, had ceased to run while he pursued and *might*, horrible thought, now chase *him*!

Seeing me, perhaps in the form of a Deliverer, The Blackness, in obvious relief, rushed up to me, the hare made off, and I sank down upon a tree stump and greatly offended my little man by my immoderate laughter.

That hour and a half of liberty and joy for him must never be lost, for the rest of the day must be spent in captivity (save for short and anxious sorties on the lead), and therefore I rejoiced that he expended so much energy in his beloved woods that he was generally glad and grateful to relax and snoozle peacefully on my divan bed — very seldom in the large rush basket — when we came home. Luckily Kitty adored him, so that I could safely leave him with her when unexpected work suddenly presented itself.

London was being intensively bombed, and more and more homeless people must be housed — somewhere. The wife of our Member, young and full of initiative, conceived the idea of hiring and equipping every large empty country house in the neighbourhood and filling it with these tragic families. Sussex was not, she knew, the ideal county for such a scheme, being the fighting area for our aeroplanes which strove nightly over our heads to intercept the German planes that crossed the coast, only twenty miles away, and roared over us on their way to London. But the need was urgent; there were many large empty houses, with prolific gardens which could be cultivated to produce vegetables for the hungry multitude, and therefore this warm-hearted and enterprising woman went ahead with her scheme, and soon after its inception, roped me in to help her. After all, we argued, it was one chance in a hundred that the bombs from an escaping German plane should be unloaded upon our protégées, though very often they were showered down upon the surrounding countryside to lighten the enemy plane and to enable it to soar out of the reach of a pursuing Spitfire; and we hoped fervently that, during battle, wounded planes of neither nationality would crash in flames upon our roofs.

I shall never forget the first instalment of refugees who arrived before the house that was to receive them could be fully equipped. Beds there were, and roaring open fires had been lit to welcome them, but there were but a few wooden benches drawn up around a trestle table in the large room which was to serve as a communal dining-room. On those hard benches weary mothers huddled in depressed silence while their grimy, white-faced children raced and screamed through the rooms of the house. *They*, young with effervescing spirits, seemed to enjoy a new experience, but their mothers, worn out with sleeplessness and nights spent in crowded airless shelters while hell was let loose above them, nearly all wore a dazed and hopeless expression. A few indomitable women were squabbling for priority of use of the one small gas stove we had been able to procure, and from their bundles were unpacking battered saucepans and frying pans. Others, who had been defeated in the struggle, complained bitterly that with only *one* gas cooker for so large a quantity of people how was anyone ever going to get a kettle boiling to make a comforting cup of tea? It amazed me that it occurred to no one that a kettle boils quickest over a blazing log fire, and that bacon and eggs and sausages can also be cooked in the same manner. There were good fires in every room and plenty of kettles. These women were all so accustomed to the system of the slot-meter that they were quite helpless and hopeless when they could no longer slip in a coin and be provided at once with gas and electricity for their cooking.

Their benefactress, trying to explain, through the din made by the children, that in a few days everything would be organised and a capable canteen cook supplied to feed the household, cast a despairing look at me.

"What can we do *at once* to make them settle down?" she whispered.

"MUSIC," I said firmly. "A wireless — a gramaphone — a penny whistle — *anything!*"

Although we needed comfortable chairs, more cooking utensils and many more practical and useful things, she had the vision to see at once what I meant. In the London air raid shelters every one sang "Roll out the barrel" and other heartening songs, and the cosiness of communal singing kept away the horrors.

So music was magically procured, and its result was equally magical. Knitting was produced from bundles, tongues were loosened, neighbourly gossip was exchanged between complete strangers; the younger women, tired as they were, actually rose to their swollen feet and danced when the first notes of a jazz band came upon the air.

My suggestion was a great success, and it inspired other ideas in the brains of the few refugee fathers of the party. One knew a friend who possessed a little home cinematograph. He could surely be persuaded to lend it to amuse the children, and perhaps I could get into touch with the Ministry of Education, or some such association, to provide films to teach the children something while arrangements were being made for them to attend schools. Another father shyly told me that he was considered a bit of a nib at gardening, and asked if he might try to tidy up the neglected grounds of the house. The women, he suggested, might do the weeding if he and his pals (under the influence of that blaring music which was torturing my ear-drums the other refugee papas had already become "pals") did the heavy digging. The "pals," so lately strangers had drawn near and assented eagerly to his proposals; one was a mason, out of work, and he became ambitious to create a rockery and to build bird baths.

The atmosphere was fast becoming cosy and "matey." Even the children seemed to feel that this house was becoming "a home from home," and proved it by making indiscriminate pools all over the parquet floor whenever Nature urged them to do so. Reproof at that moment was unthinkable. Neither I nor my companion had the heart to be "governessy." All those little matters could be righted gradually. For the moment all we must provide was a certain degree of comfort and the maximum amount of cheeriness. The Cockney morale is notoriously marvellous, and that priceless sense of humour must be revived at once.

I could not be shocked when a buxom young woman came up to me and cheekily said:

"Look 'ere, missus, ef the weather gets colder we shall want more blankets on our beds than wot we've got. An' ef we don't get 'em we shall 'ave to get in the troops to keep us warm at night."

Both I and my companion told her and the laughing women around her that they were at liberty to resort to this extreme measure IF, by to-morrow night, we had not supplied sufficient blankets for everybody. They were supplied.

I knew by the searching look that she gave us after making this sally that it was merely a test. If we didn't blink, if the expression of our eyes did not become cold and steely, nor our mouths suddenly become spring traps, then we had humour and humanity, and might henceforth be treated as friends. We were. I am happy to say that both of us passed that test, and that afterwards our visits were welcomed and our advice sought — and sometimes followed.

On the whole we were very fortunate in our evacuees. Of course we did have difficulties and a few unpleasant and discontented people who could never be satisfied or had mischief-making tongues. But we had very few who preferred to return to blazing bombs and fish and chips and cinemas rather than enjoy a less dangerous life amid the downs and woods of one of England's loveliest counties.

Eternal human nature is to me the most fascinating and absorbing of all studies; the love of it inherited, perhaps, from my extraordinary little mother, who confessed that she would far rather visit a London slum and talk to its inhabitants than be shown the glories of architecture seen in one of our noble cathedrals.

"LIFE interests me vividly. PEOPLE — their lives and their struggles — the development of their children — THE PRESENT — THE FUTURE. For me THE PAST is depressing — dead — over and done with — dusty and sad."

The lives and interests and problems of these evacuees from London helped me at that time sometimes to forget my anxiety for *Mademoiselle* and my friends in France who might suffer even a worse fate and be subjected to enemy occupation. Thank God our R.A.F. had so far saved us from that dread horror.

CHAPTER
EIGHT

The Savoury Soup

To me, for the remainder of my life, those days of peril during and after the Battle of Britain will ever be marked in my memory by a great glorious golden triumphant cross. It was wonderful to feel English fighting blood surging in one's veins; it was even more wonderful to feel oneself a member of so great a family; for the nation had, for once, become just that, with its King and Queen as father and mother, their hearts full of love, understanding and compassion for all their suffering children. Gone was all snobbery and class distinction; formalities and rules of conduct were swept away by the common danger. We were all in the same soup, a lovely savoury soup with the vulgar onion (without which no soup is worth a sup) flavouring the consommé — an unusual mixture, but new and interesting.

There was a warm atmosphere of friendliness everywhere. In buses, noble ladies swung on straps, and smiled sweetly if wanly when their feet were trodden upon. In the first-class carriages of trains, invaded by holders of third-class tickets, those who had paid the true fare in the hope of gaining peace and privacy no longer looked at the invading mob as though they were *poisson pourri,* but squeezed themselves into nothingness to enable weary people to sit down, and then entered into sympathetic conversation with them. Never being sure of seeing anyone again made every one kinder and far more careful in speech with their friends and their dependants; for when you said good-bye or good night to anyone, you could never be sure that he — or you — might not be blown into eternity by a bomb before morning. During and after an air raid the houses of all survivors became at once homes for the homeless. That period was the nearest approach to the millennium that England has ever reached. Lions *did* lie down with lambs; all kinds of funny beasts came out of their lairs in the spirit of friendliness, and gaily plumaged birds of paradise fluttered happily among the sparrows of the slums. It was refreshing to hear the Countess of X laughingly telling her friends of a remark made by a very small urchin, lodged with a mass of other waifs from dockland in her great castle. As she entered a room which had been transformed into a dormitory he pointed at her and observed in a hoarse but very audible whisper to a newcomer in the next bed:

"That's the bloody old bitch wot gives us the chocklits."

Her husband, also very popular with the children, went by an even worse name preceded by the same adjective and also beginning with B, and he was very proud of it.

We all became much more human. We also made startling discoveries. It took a war and a few showers of bombs thrown upon slum areas to lay bare hidden horrors of housing which should have been impossible in an England of the twentieth century. We had many salutary shocks and were temporarily shaken out of our self-complacency. There is now a hope that we may in future be less smug and selfish.

Funny things happened all the time. It gave me a tremendous kick to enter the office of a great personage during a London air raid and to find her on all fours, having just submitted to the urgent advice of her secretary that she should shelter under a solid office table. We often became frogs at that time. It was all very cosy, squatting in shelters of this description and exchanging experiences between bombs and the ear-splitting but reassuring crash and thunder of our defensive barrage. And how stimulating the cup of tea brewed afterwards to steady frayed nerves. What GALLONS of tea must have been drunk in England during the war, and the highest consumption must certainly have been in the days of the Battle of Britain.

I remember seeing a band of men outside the Hyde Park Hotel digging out a huge unexploded time-bomb. The staff of the hotel came out with a large metal tray loaded with cups of tea to hearten the workers, who stopped work and gratefully, without hurry, imbibed it, standing around that bomb which was liable to explode at any moment. The photographer of some newspaper passing just then in search of sensational pictures, paused and took a snapshot of the little scene. I expect he thought, as I did, that it was a good illustration of the British *sang-froid*, and well worth the risk of a moment's pause in that dangerous area.

Dignity and conventions were blasted away by bombs. Who could look dignified descending the staircase of an hotel during a sudden raid, in the company of other guests of both sexes, wearing sketchy night attire, with a pencil held between the teeth and a pillow upon the head?

That devil blast had a grotesque and ghastly sense of humour. No one could ever predict what fantastic thing he would do next. A pretty débutante was dining in the bow window of a small but select restaurant behind Piccadilly with a rather severe and starchy great-uncle. Suddenly he found himself, clad only in his shirt, seated on the pavement of the street opposite his niece, whose young loveliness was scarcely veiled by a very diaphanous chemise, surrounded by the débris of the bow window and their half-consumed dinner.

Now, how could he continue to look severe and starchy after that? When their bruises were healed could they *both* laugh and enjoy that memory? One hopes so.

CHAPTER
NINE

The Stop-Cock

Winter came upon us, a very hard winter, and snow fell so thickly in my valley that the precipice path leading to the main road threatened to become impassable. Mercifully one of the two gardeners living in the lodges at the top had been "reserved for agriculture" and the local fire service, when the other was swept away into the R.A.F. The faithful Fred, who remained, trudged through the soft deep snow, brought my rations and shovelled away the drifts around the cottage when his work for the Big House was ended. But life became so difficult that at last I listened to the advice of my friends and accepted the invitation of one of them to share her bungalow on the top of the cliff until a thaw set in and liberated my cottage.

I had met her in the South of France whither she had gone with the firm resolve to buy or build for herself a dream house in Provence. The outbreak of war temporarily frustrated that dream, and when forced to return to England she came to see me, fell in love with my surroundings, and subsequently begged my landlord to find her some perching place on his estate. Laughingly he told her that the only corner he could think of was a little house built by a previous millionaire-owner of the property for his Great Danes. These kennels stood on the edge of the great rock cliff above my valley, overlooking the five little lakes. The roof of "Many Waters" could just be seen. My friend and I saw possibilities in these kennels, for the Great Danes had been luxuriously housed, each in his own room lit by electric light and opening into a slip of a room furnished with a sink and a cooking stove to facilitate feeding and the daily toilet of the dogs. An architect was summoned, and when a partition or two had been knocked down, a bay window thrown out, a bathroom added and other modern conveniences installed, those dog kennels were transformed into a tiny but most convenient dwelling. I will henceforth refer to its tenant as the "Lady of the Kennels." Into its minute spare bedroom The Blackness and I tucked ourselves. He complained that the bed was not so wide as OURS, but it wouldn't be so bad because the weather was bitterly cold, and he could always lie on the top of me and we could thus keep each other warm. This idea he put into practice. We were all very cosy, because the walls were so thin that conversation could be carried on with anyone within the house without raising the voice.

One morning, after the hardest frost we yet had had, while I was picking off small icicles hanging from the *inside* of my window-frame above my bed, I heard the voice of the faithful Fred. He was asking my hostess to inform her ladyship that something in the pipe line had burst in her cottage, which was now flooding fast. Apparently the ram, which automatically supplied the Big House and all the cottages on the estate with water, continued to pump it into mine, so that as fast as he baled the water out of the kitchen it filled up again. Needless to say, it was Sunday. Why do all pipes burst, all chimneys catch fire, all electric lights fuse and all such domestic crises always occur on the Sabbath day, when plumbers, electricians, chimney-sweeps and other magicians are taking their well-earned rest or recreation.

"I'll dress quickly and come down, Fred," I called through the roars of rage of The Blackness. "Surely every house has something called a stop-cock? We'll search for mine."

Hurriedly I threw on clothes, put on my Alpine boots, and leaving the Black One in the care of his adopted aunt, the Lady of the Kennels, ploughed through the snow with Fred. It was tricky work finding the stone stairway, and before we could pass on we were obliged to knock clotted snow from the branches of exotic shrubs which in spring are laden with gorgeous blossom and now completely barred our path. Frost had made the steps slippery, and we both of us narrowly escaped several falls. Another amusing adventure. And when at length we had shuffled our way to my back door and entered the little kitchen, I laughed still more. For all my blue saucepans had been washed from their moorings and were bobbing about like merry little ships on a troubled sea. With every pulsing beat of that dam ram a fresh wave of water washed into the kitchen, emptying my cupboards of their contents.

Fred's dismay was intense. "I baled out all the water before I came up to tell your ladyship — and now look at it!" he growled.

"The stop-cock!" I reminded him. "Can it be that big

tap near the floor in the downstairs W.C., Fred? The flood seems to be coming from there." Rolling up our trousers we waded through that icy water.

I was right. That big tap *was* the saving stop-cock, BUT — it was the stop-cock that had burst in the frost . . . !

There was nothing for it but for one of us to remain in the cottage baling frantically while the other climbed the precipice and telephoned for a plumber — any plumber. The valiant Fred offered to do this, and I was left fighting the flood alone. I opened the kitchen door, and with a broom directed the water outside, impeded badly by a raised door-sill. It seemed untold ages — though really only an hour — before I most thankfully heard male voices in the distance, and soon the gallant old plumber appeared with Fred. First he suggested stopping the ram, but a vision of fifty unwashed babies in the Big House and the inconvenience which would be caused to all the inhabitants in the little houses on the estate caused me to forbid this solution to my watery problem. Surely he could do one of the magic things plumbers do to save the situation? I don't know what he did, but he did it, and the surface of the sea within my house ceased to be troubled, the agitated saucepans careered less wildly and, thank Heaven, the waves had not yet washed into my dining-room next door to the kitchen because, mercifully, it was built on a higher level. There was now nothing left to be done save more energetic baling, followed by swabbing and the work of salvage. OH . . . ! My cupboards . . . !

Thanking Fred warmly, I assured him that now, with

the plumber's aid, I could cope with the situation, and bidding him return to his own manifold duties at once, I put myself under the orders of the Man of Pipes.

He stationed me by the kitchen door with my broom, and, seizing another, he began to swash great tidal waves in my direction, which I obediently hurried on into the garden. But he had the strong arms of a man, and he hadn't been swashing icy water out of the house for an hour, as I had. We started our work with rhythmic precision, and at first I managed to keep up with him, but ere long my efforts began to flag and his waves overwhelmed me, washing above and *into* my high boots. He was not hampered by a raised door-sill as I was, and what with his regular waves and the backwash of mine from that maddening ridge of wood, I got wetter and wetter, and my efforts more and more feeble because, of course, I began to laugh. I laughed and laughed and laughed, silently and helplessly, until my broom fell from powerless frozen hands.

Not until his waves returned upon him, so intent upon his work was he, did the old plumber realise that his assistant had stopped work. Then he straightened up, gave me one glance, and his impassive old face broke into a wide slow grin.

"You're not accustomed to this kind of a job, my lady?" he suggested ironically.

"You know I've called this cottage 'Many Waters'?" I retorted relevantly. Then he, too, temporarily dropped his broom, and many waters became laughing water.

CHAPTER
TEN

The Flaming Sword

The following spring, such a mixture of beauty, splendour and agony for England, will haunt my memory till I die. The poor words of men and women could never depict the glory of gallantry shown by our airmen; the magnificent spirit of our civilians; that tense happy comradeship which a common danger always brings; and so, as it seemed to me, Nature endeavoured to paint it all for those who had eyes to see. Never have I seen such a wealth of blossom, heralded by the first pale primroses in the woods, which later were so thickly carpeted with bluebells that the azure sky above them seemed almost grey in contrast. Then the azaleas and rhododendrons burst into flower; the old apple trees around the lake foamed into bloom, and were reflected like a design of lace on the silver water beneath. "Many Waters" was surrounded with blossom, it seemed to stand in the midst of a Brobdingnagian flower show — colour flooded the heights and streamed over the rocks into the valley and the air was heavy with scent. Mating birds chanted, rabbits curveted, the grass slopes were studded with flickering white bob-tails; the very atmosphere seemed to pulse with life and anticipation.

Something of this general excitement communicated itself to my Blackness, whose soft brilliant eyes, pink tongue and waggling little body seemed all of them to plead with me to set him free to race amid all this beauty. Early in the morning he would wake me by padding along my bed till he reached the pillow, then stand over me with his head on one side and one banner ear brushing my cheek, and when I looked into his eyes I read there that urgent question, "Oh, WILL you take me out?" And because of those red terrors I could not (except for little runs around the cottage attached to a lead). He would trot over to the window, stand up on his hind legs and peer out into the dewy freshness of the woods. Sometimes a brace of partridges would be bustling about the clear spaces between forests of bracken. These interested him, for he had seen no game in Provence, but only when a rabbit scudded across the grass did he give tongue, short shrill yelps, a tense little black body and then, as he saw its white bob-tail disappearing, an hysterical howl of frustration. I often wondered which of us suffered the most during those moments.

Sometimes it was too much for us, and, greatly daring, we risked a sortie during the danger hours. But it was unnerving. "Many Waters" lay in its ventriloquial valley surrounded by rock cliffs. Often we would be in the depths of the woods, The Blackness, in chase of some bird or beast, lost to us and deaf to whistle or call, when suddenly the concerted roars of the red terrors would sound close upon us. Then my knees turned to water, and I felt physically sick, and the complexion of my companion paled; for we realised that two powerful dogs, undisciplined and wearing no collars, could overpower and savage one little cocker spaniel which they considered as a trespasser on THEIR estate. Even if we could scale the rocks and reach the scene of battle before tragedy overcame him, how could we hold two strong, enraged and collarless dogs? And often those dogs, although they seemed to be in the woods, would only be racing about on the lawns of the Big House half a mile away — had we but known! The hatred of red Romulus for Dominie had increased with time. He paid visits to the cottage, marking, as is the unpleasant way of male dogs, the front door and the corners of the house as HIS, then tearing up the turf with strong defiant kicks and scrapes. This behaviour always sent the poor little imprisoned Blackness frantic. He rushed from room to room, screaming with rage, and watched from the windows this scene of desecration of what he considered HIS domain, while red Romulus outside roared insults till all was pandemonium. The windows of "Many Waters" were very near the ground and opened as casements, so that there was the continual fear that if we left one open to air the house, Dominie would leap from it to confront or go in search of his enemy, for he had courage, he was extremely possessive and, alas! aggressive.

One evening the mule-bell rang outside. I shouted to Kitty to make sure that Dominie was shut up somewhere before she opened the front door, because the visitor was probably my landlord, who often strolled down from the Big House on his return from the City to laugh and talk a while with me, almost always accompanied by the dogs.

The Blackness was in the hall, and Kitty unwisely ignored my warning, thinking that if she opened the door just a crack, keeping a leg across it, this would be enough. But she had not realised the great strength of Romulus, that huge imperial red setter, rendered stronger by the lust to get at his enemy. With one leap he had forced open the door, nearly knocking Kitty over, rushed round The Blackness and seized his hind leg in his great jaws. In a second I had swept my Blackness, struggling and yelling with fury, into my arms, and my large landlord had grasped Romulus by the scruff of his neck. Mercifully the teeth of an old dog are not usually good, and he hadn't had time to get a good grip. Fortunately, also, the bitch was not present or she would have attacked with her male. Romulus was hurled outside and the door barred. I sank into an armchair, still clasping my Blackness to my bumping heart — my knees would no longer support me.

My landlord, having made his apologies, stood regarding me, silently and with interest, mopping his brow.

"The heel of Achilles," he murmured, with a twinkle. "The wonderful Lady of the Lake who isn't afraid of bombs, or of solitary nocturnal walks in the woods where German spies or parachutists might well lurk — who lives in a secluded cottage with no telephone — who seemed to me to have no nerves . . . !"

I licked my dry lips and said shakily:

"Yes — Dominie — you see, he is so precious. Elisabeth — *Mademoiselle* — gave him to me; he's all I've got left of my home in Provence. Well, the danger is safely over — this time — and now let us go up into my studio and relax."

When we were seated comfortably before the fire in my lovely restful room I pleaded again for more liberty for my poor little man.

"You've seen for yourself that Romulus's one idea is to kill him," I urged.

My landlord looked uncomfortable. "You could put him into that little wired-in chicken run at the back, couldn't you? You see, I'm in the City all day and mother is alone and likes to wander about the property with her dogs. She's given up her house to the L.C.C. and if she can't even walk about her own grounds with her dogs whenever she likes — well — she would have a grievance against life."

"Couldn't your dogs sometimes be shut into those lovely wired-in runs on the terrace?" I suggested.

"I'm afraid not," he replied, "because the refugee children tease them — throw in little pebbles and so on. The *only* safe time is the hour and a half we arranged when they come indoors to be fed. We have no staff left to speak of, and there'd be nobody responsible to see that the dogs were shut up at any other time."

I saw that it was hopeless any longer to plead the cause of Dominie, and he lay at my feet and regarded me mournfully.

Hatherway had confided to me one day that old Romulus was gun-shy, and that if I carried a rook rifle when I went for walks with Dominie and fired it into the air if we met Romulus, he would surely flee in terror. Unfortunately I also am gun-shy, though up

74

to now I have succeeded in concealing this fact, but I decided at once that for the defence of my Blackness I must buy a gun and, if necessary, fire it. So I drove into East Grinstead, and at the gunsmith's shop, which has since become a crater, I bought a little rifle. He warned me before I purchased it that during the war he was not permitted to sell me live ammunition, and seemed surprised by my fervent "Thank God!" He asked me then, very courteously and gently, of what use a gun would be to me *without* ammunition? And when I replied: "I only want blank — to frighten a dog," he had some difficulty in retaining his gravity, but at once said, "Oh! — If *that's* all —" shovelled some cartridges from a drawer, and proceeded to extract bullets from them as though he were pulling out teeth. He then explained the mechanism of the gun, and how to put on the safety catch so that if I stumbled in the woods it wouldn't go off, handed me the infernal machine with a smile and a bow, and wished me good hunting. No doubt behind that suave manner he was hiding merriment and thinking me all sorts of a fool. If he was, then I entirely agreed with him; for, being useless with gadgets and mechanical contrivances, it was more than likely that in a moment of crisis I should pull the push or push the pull of that horrible instrument of death and terror now posed on the back seat of the car.

Thenceforth on all our woodland walks we were impeded by the weight of the gun, and very funny we must have looked. Indeed my landlord's mother found the sight of us starting for our walks, as seen from the Big House above, so amusing that she drew one of her very clever caricatures, depicting the Lady of the Kennels and myself trousered and wearing huge hats, one of us carrying the gun while the other towed a diminutive black dog on a lead. In the top left-hand corner of the picture was a large medallion encircling the smiling face of red Romulus. This amusing *chef-d'oeuvre* was entitled "Mirage." She did not wish to believe that my terror for Dominie was a very real — and justified — thing.

The crisis came when one day, having business to do, I took Dominie with me in the car. There was a letter to be delivered at the Big House, and so I left the car in the main road some distance from the entrance gates — carefully shut the windows and locked him in while I walked up the drive. The red terrors roared out to meet me, and I had a friendly little talk with them before delivering my letter, but unfortunately, I suppose smelling the fresh scent of their enemy on my clothes, they followed me back to the car. Dominie saw them, reared up on his hind legs, bristling. I had only time to slip into the car and slam the door before both dogs fell upon the car, roaring and battering at the windows, which I feared at any moment might break. It was like seeing a moving picture of what would happen to my Blackness if ever they caught him in the woods — rolling eyes, bared fangs and slavering mouths. Some guests of my landlord's, walking in the grounds and hearing the hideous din, rushed out to discover the cause. It took two strong men to draw those dogs off the car, and neither of them looked as though he enjoyed the effort.

After this I drove into the grounds of a neighbouring

estate, stopped the engine, got out of the car with Dominie safely attached to a lead, sank down under a great tree in a secluded spot hugging him to my heart — and — howled.

I don't cry easily, and never before witnesses, but I had just seen the flaming sword barring me from the little English paradise I had found for my Blackness and for me. I loved the little house in the woods, and the quiet beauty around me satisfied my soul, but I realised that I could no longer live in such a state of tension — and it wasn't fair to Dominie. We must lose one more home, and go in search of some other habitation — and it nearly broke my heart to contemplate such an exile.

I suppose, as I sat under that tree, that I must have been sending up voiceless prayers to be helped to a solution of the problem. Anyway, when the time came it was solved for me.

CHAPTER
ELEVEN

I Meet Richard

I had an invitation to luncheon one day from the friend in East Grinstead who had recommended the clever vet for my Blackness. She told me that one of the young airmen, who was being treated by the "wizard" plastic surgeon for terrible injuries, was very anxious to meet me.

"To meet *me*?" I echoed. "Do I know him?"

"No, but he has read your books. He wants to write and doesn't know how to begin; he wants to talk to you," she replied. In general I refused social invitations, but this was one that must be fulfilled, and I accepted it at once, the more readily because The Blackness was also included.

On the day appointed, the weather being fine and the grass dry, I was able to drive my little car down the precipice and up to the door of "Many Waters," so that Dominie could leap straight into the car without risk.

Groomed and shining and sleek he waltzed madly round every room in the cottage, frantic with joy that he was to be allowed to come with his mother, then scrambled into his seat, where he sat quivering with excitement, looking out of the corners of his eyes at Kitty, as if defying her to remove him.

Our drive was happy and uneventful until we had nearly reached our destination, and then we both narrowly escaped a violent end. A dispatch-rider suddenly roared past us on his motor bicycle, his exhaust firing three pistol shots as he came alongside. The Blackness went mad with terror. Was the horror of France, so nearly forgotten, to come upon him again? He leaped on to the steering wheel, then down on the floor, struggling to hide beneath my legs and getting mixed up in the steering gear and brake. A Baby Austin is but a cockle-shell with a finger-touch steering, and his sudden and unexpected impact on the wheel caused the car to swerve violently across the road. There was a grinding shriek of brakes, and a gigantic army lorry behind us nearly caught my running-board. I had just time to see the soldier-driver shake his fist at me as he passed and accelerated up the hill. I drew up at the side of the road and tried to calm my poor little black man, but chocolate and charcoal biscuits were of no use at all. He hid his nose under my arm and shook as though with ague. Luckily I had allowed plenty of time for our drive, and after a little spell of quiet and caressing I realised that his thoughts must be changed. We were on a steep hill with rocky banks shaded by great beech trees. Among those gnarled roots *might* lurk rabbits. We would go and see. We snuffed, and then scrabbled for a bit, and gradually that unknown terror passed away and we could resume our drive, with The Blackness secured by a short lead to the door handle.

There is a mystery that I have never fathomed. The back-firing of a motor bicycle always sent Dominie, so terribly sensitive to all sudden sharp noises, into paroxysms of terror. But if a sporting gun was loosed off in his proximity he merely held up an alert head, and his eager spaniel eyes seemed to ask me to give him an order. He always felt that something was expected of him, and was keenly anxious to do it. No terror, not even a start of surprise.

Finding a little girl dog when we reached our destination made him finally forget the shock he had had. Together they raced madly over the sloping lawns of a lovely safe enclosed garden while we had luncheon.

I was shown into a large room where the guests were already assembled, and introductions followed. With his back to the room, silhouetted against a sunlit window, stood the tall lithe figure of a young man. He was talking to our host, who turned to me and said as I approached:

"Lady Fortescue, this is Richard Hillary, who was so anxious to meet you."

During the war one had been inured to bearing the sight of tragic disfigurements, but this beautiful boy — for one could see that he *had* been beautiful — his figure, his hands, his fair wavy hair — those blazing blue eyes still were. But his face had only just been grafted — eyelids had been added which were dead white in a bronzed face and held in place by a talc frame, half a lip had been added — the same dead white — one arm braced upon a kind of tennis-racket contrivance with loops on the rounded frame to straighten crooked fingers immersed too long in tannic acid. The other hand with some fingers burned off.

He wheeled towards me, and stood with his gallant head thrown back and the bright sunlight shining full upon that marred face, the burning blue eyes, streaming from strain, staring defiantly into mine.

"Look well at me," they seemed to say. "But damn you, don't you DARE to pity me." I was being tested. Thank God I passed that test.

He sat next to me at luncheon, and we talked of this and that. I longed to help him with his eating implements, but he had already told me without words that he was to be treated as a normal person, and he managed clumsily alone while I talked of other things than the war.

"Our hostess told me that you are keen to start writing," I ventured, as, so far, he hadn't mentioned this subject. "She said that you wanted to talk to me about it, but that would be quite impossible here. Personally, I can never talk seriously in a crowd; I'm too shy and I can't concentrate. With half an ear I'm listening to scraps of other people's conversation, and my mind plays gymnastics."

"I'm like that," he said, with a quick look of sympathetic understanding.

"But if you'd come and visit me in my cottage in the woods we should hear only our own voices and the sound of many waters." A curious stillness seemed suddenly to enfold him. He had ceased to use his poor hands; he stopped eating and stared silently at his plate. Then he looked straight into my eyes and said, in a very quiet tone but with great emphasis, "Oh, I *should* like to do that! But" — with a helpless gesture — "lack of transport. Do you live far away? How could I get to you?"

There being a pause in the general conversation at that moment, his question was overheard by our hostess.

"Lady Fortescue has chosen the loveliest and most inaccessible part of Sussex. She lives in a cottage at the bottom of a precipice in the woods of a private estate with no road approaching it. But I have to attend a committee in that direction in a fortnight's time, and I could drive you to the lodge gates on the main road, and you can make the perilous descent."

"That sounds to me a very attractive programme," said Richard, and we fixed that engagement a fortnight ahead. He was to come to tea with me and my Blackness, who rushed pantingly in at that moment with his lady friend and was formally introduced.

When I got home I marked that date on my calendar with a red cross, wondering as I did so whether that gallant boy would remember — or forget. The young forget so easily, their impressionable minds retain so much that only very vivid impressions remain in the foreground. This boy was staying in the house of a millionaire, transformed during the war into a convalescent home for airmen, who were spoiled and entertained most lavishly by the owners. Probably something much more amusing would be planned for him on that afternoon, and, after all, our engagement was a full fortnight ahead. Nevertheless on the day appointed I gave Kitty an afternoon off. I was so afraid that if he did come she might not be able to conceal her feelings when she saw him — and she was engaged to a boy in the Air Force. Then I laid the table for two in my tiny dining-room adjoining the kitchen, lit a cheerful log fire in my studio — and waited.

Precisely at four p.m. the front door was smartly rapped by the old Sussex horse-shoe I had fixed there, and I ran downstairs to open it. Outside stood a tall figure muffled in an overcoat of Air Force blue. Richard Hillary!

"Oh, I *am* so glad you remembered!" I cried eagerly.

"I was terrified *you* would have forgotten!" he replied.

"Well, we DIDN'T, did we?" I said, welcoming him into my little hall and, having realised his savage resolve to be independent, *not* offering to help him to take off his overcoat.

"We're quite alone," I went on. "It is my maiden's day out, so we must make our own picnic tea. Will you make the toast while I fuss with the kettle and things in the kitchen."

"Right, but I shall probably burn it," he said, awkwardly picking up the toasting-fork.

"I have never yet *not* burned toast," I consoled him, "but a coal fire is safer — because slower — than an electric contrivance in which the toast invariably goes up in flames if you turn your back on it for a moment."

Shyness disappears so much more quickly if you are doing things with your hands. While I scalded mine making the tea, Richard Hillary scorched the toast, for he began to talk of his recent experiences as though to an old friend, and clean forgot what he was supposed to be doing. We had a funny tea; we could neither of us open a tin of chicken paste sealed for export — I am perfectly useless with gadgets, and his poor hands prevented him from coping with it.

"I can't tell you how it consoles me to see a *man* helpless with a gadget," I laughed at him. "I haven't got a pick-axe, so let's scrounge in the larder and see what we can find."

We found some honey, with which we armed ourselves happily, for it is quite impossible to eat either honey or Mr. Lyle's famous gold syrup without becoming sticky more or less everywhere. Holes in the bread betray one, and the transit of a spoonful from pot to plate is very tricky. However, we rinsed ourselves under the tap of the kitchen sink, gave the sulky Blackness his saucer of tea (he always *hated* guests of mine in HIS house because my attention was diverted from HIM), and then we went upstairs to my studio.

Richard stood just inside the door and surveyed the little interior without speaking. His eyes travelled from the glowing fire of logs to my large writing-table near the window, noted the bowl of spring flowers near Mummie's portrait, travelled to the bookcase with the picture of my John above it, to the glass-paned door leading to loveliness outside, and my many-cushioned divan bed with a dent in the middle where the small black body of The Blackness had lain, and the picture of Dürer's Praying Hands hung over it. He looked at the lovely shepherd's crook, made by a shepherd of the Sussex Downs, the unframed oblong mirrors on the walls reflecting glimpses of ferns and trees from the window; the soft green carpet-like forest grass, and the rude cross made of silver birch logs hanging near the door. Then he said a most unexpected thing.

"For years I have been looking for the Circles of Peace. This is the centre of the Circles of Peace."

Then he sank into an armchair, and with a rapt look on his face just listened.

"You hear only the sound of running water," he said under his breath.

"I heard the sound of many waters when I first saw this place, and so, of course, I called it that."

"'Many Waters.' A perfect name," he murmured to himself. The Blackness broke that silence by galloping upstairs, and seeing Richard seated in one of HIS chairs, roaring at him indignantly. A charcoal biscuit pacified him and he leaped on to my divan, where he curled himself up and lay with his banner ears spread out and his eyes firmly fixed on me. After that, conversation could be resumed on more normal lines. We talked of the war, and he told me of his experiences, his terrible smash and all he had suffered, and was suffering, in various hospitals, dwelling on this very lightly if sometimes a little bitterly, but always with an ironic smile.

"I fear the first sight of me after the smash must have been a bit of a shock to my mother, for I was rather a mess, but she didn't show it, bless her — she's rather an extraordinary person, my mother; I can treat her like a contemporary, and even if she can't approve the things I say or do, at any rate she never fails to see the other fellow's point of view. No, she NEVER fails. She's got vision — and she can hit out from the shoulder." He chuckled to himself gently. "I was rather nice to look at once, and I suppose getting a bit uppish and spoiled. She told me in hospital that perhaps this accident had saved me from becoming a cad."

I experienced a keen and instant desire to meet Mrs. Hillary.

"I believe I could write here," said Richard after another listening silence. "Only the eternal sound of that running water, and now the note of that sleepy bird. How clever of you to find this place. That luxurious mansion in Grinstead is always filled with a lot of other chaps chattering — wireless and gramophones blaring away. It's like the monkey house at the Zoo. No one could do serious work there. I do *want* to write. Somehow I feel I've got to write — but what about? How? When and where?"

"Write about all the things you've been telling me," I said urgently; "all that and more. You made me see it all so vividly that I can never forget some of that horror. If you write that story only half as well as you told it, your book will be read all over the world."

"If I speak the truth about lots of things I'd be shot out of the Service, and certainly never admitted into another hospital," he chortled. "I'm the *enfant terrible* wherever I'm sent. I'm a damned nuisance too, because I'm a rebel at heart, and I refuse to keep silly rules. If I want to go out and enjoy myself, why shouldn't I go? If I want a drink — lots of drinks — why shouldn't I have 'em? I'm certain of one thing — that repressions and inhibitions and rules and regulations and red tape never did anyone any good. I believe in the liberty of the individual." He gave me a wicked twinkling look to see how I was taking all this, and observing the elevated right eyebrow and a mocking light in the eye, observed:

"You and my mother must get together. You'd understand each other. And I say, if I give you the address of someone, and she writes to you, I wonder if you'd ask her down here to stay with you. It's just what she needs — this place and you. I'm worried about her. She's talking of shutting herself up in a convent and becoming a nun — just because she's had a bad time — she'll tell you all about it when she comes, I'm sure of that." He scribbled a name and address on my writing pad, muttering as he did so, "What a waste! What a nun!"

"Do you think she will write to me?" I asked. "I'd love to have her here."

"Yes, she will," he said emphatically. But "Denise" never did.

"I've ordered a taxi to take me back at six. The quaint chap who generally shoves for us had to take someone across Sussex, so can't fetch me this evening," Richard informed me. "He's awfully good to us all; drives us all over Sussex, and when we ask the fare he says 'One shilling and sixpence'! Clever chap, educated and all that; can't always have been a chauffeur of taxis; bit of a philosopher; seems to have adopted us all, and behaves rather like a severe nanny to me, lectures and all that. Good chap. You must meet our Mr. Baker one day. You'd appreciate him."

The mule-bell rang outside the front door at that moment.

"I'm afraid that's my taxi-man," said Richard sadly, and we went downstairs to open the door.

"How on earth did *you* get back in time?" he exclaimed

in astonishment. "You're the other side of Sussex! I expected another chap to come and fetch me. Lady Fortescue, this is Mr. Baker after all!"

"Do you imagine that I'd allow a rip like you out on your own with night coming on?" answered Mr. Baker as we shook hands. "I've come to conduct you safely back to your nice little bed."

Thenceforth Mr. Baker and I became great friends. He was a kind of Admirable Crichton. His life had been embittered, but although disillusioned he refused to be crushed by misfortune. When others were in trouble of any sort, mental, physical, or mechanical, he was always ready to give the safest advice and the swiftest, most intelligent aid, for beneath that somewhat acrid manner beat a warm and generous heart.

Thank you — for lots of things — dear Mr. Baker. . . . Before Richard left I begged him to feel that whenever he wanted to be quiet, to think over his book or to make notes, he could always come to my cottage.

"Even if I'm out with The Blackness you can always let yourself in, because the key lives under that flat stone near the front door. You'll find an abundance of scribbling paper, pencils and writing paraphernalia on my desk if you want to write, and your own comfortable chair if you want to think things out. The fire is always laid ready to be lit, and it would be the cosiest thing in the world if on returning from a walk in the woods I saw smoke curling from my chimney!" I assured him. He promised to come whenever he could, but again I wondered whether he would. The young may have long, long thoughts, but they often have short memories. Still, he *had* remembered to come to-day. Nevertheless it was with joy in the weeks which followed that sometimes, as The Blackness and I returned from his riot in the woods, I *did* see smoke rising from my chimney from a fire lit by Richard Hillary.

It was some time later that one of the children from the gardeners' lodges at the top of the precipice brought me down a telephone message from Richard asking me to ring him up as soon as I could. I had been obliged to install a telephone in the porch of one of those lodges because engineers decided that the difficulties of installation in my cottage were insuperable in war-time, even if my landlord would consent to the placing of telephone poles across the loveliest corner of his property. My family hated my enforced isolation from the world, in case of bombs or illness, and this telephone on the top of the precipice (quite useless in such an emergency) was really a sop for them.

So now I climbed the precipice to ring up Richard. His voice answered me, rather breathless for some reason which soon proved to be excitement.

"I've got a job! I've GOT A JOB!" he almost shouted.

"Oh Richard! What? Where? When?" I eagerly asked him.

"I'm dying to tell you all about it — the real YOU and not just a ghost-voice on this infernal though useful machine. Can I come to tea to-day?"

"Of course. Lovely! Get here as soon as you can. I'm thrilled!" I answered, then hung up the receiver, and skedaddled down the precipice to prepare for his arrival. But he never came. It grew later and later, but still no Richard, only one of the gardeners' children with yet another telephone message saying that he had been called away for an appointment with Lord Beaverbrook, and if not too late afterwards would come to see me on his way back.

Lord Beaverbrook? Something to do with the new job, no doubt. Ministry of Information? A newspaper king too. Probably Richard was to work for him — writing of a sort, but not of the kind about which he dreamed. Still, all writing is valuable experience, and even journalism teaches concentration — only so many words to a column, and space very precious. I had done it, and I knew. I longed for Richard's arrival, and when hope of it faded with the daylight, I hoped for a telephone message or a letter; but nothing came. A dead and depressing silence for days, for weeks, for months.

I never saw him again.

CHAPTER
TWELVE

"The Ark"

Just when we had got the evacuees from London contentedly tucked into several large houses, and our Member's wife had persuaded the Lady of the Kennels to undertake the work of supervising each garden, of ordering vegetable seeds and generally heartening the gardeners to outdo each other in efforts to make each house self-supporting, need I tell you that the Army commandeered each and every house, and all our work had to start again?

But also, at last, I had the longed-for message from French Headquarters in London. They told me that an association of English lovers of France had been formed, entitled *Amis des Volontaires Français*, afterwards popularly known as A.V.F. General de Gaulle was its patron, and as I was one of the earliest to offer my services to help France in any capacity, I had been taken at my word and enrolled as a member. Would I consent to be a voluntary speaker and "propagand" on platforms? I had lived in France for eleven years; I knew and loved the French, and could explain better than most people the tragic situation of seeming treachery into which they had been plunged by their politicians, and I had said that I would do ANYTHING to help France.

Yes, I had said that, and had meant it from the bottom of my heart; no drudgery would I have scorned to help my French friends. But in my wildest imaginings it had never occurred to me that I might be asked to brave the awful (to me, always awful, for I never get used to it) ordeal of speaking to crowds from public platforms. In this case the ordeal would be even more horrible because at that time so large a proportion of England was (quite naturally because it didn't understand) definitely hostile to France. To speak to a sympathetic audience is to me a great strain — and drain; therefore to talk to a hostile crowd of people, to try to soften their hearts and *make* them understand, would leave me like a sucked orange. Nevertheless, I must do it.

Now, when the Army began to occupy the houses in the neighbourhod a rumour flew around that all residents would soon be evacuated elsewhere — in a clot. Every house within the twenty-mile radius from the coast would be taken over by the Army. When I took over the lease of "Many Waters" I had been assured that my cottage was just outside that radius. Now I was informed that it lay just a few inches within it! Horrors! Bombs and aerial fighting above my head I could bear, but NOT to be evacuated in a clot.

Yet, I thought again, was not this the heaven-sent solution to my own problem, and to Dominie's? — for with Remus at large there could be no happiness or peace for him. I would evacuate myself before I was evacuated, temporarily at any rate. This new work for France would provide an object, but if I took it I must live in a corner of my own — somewhere. A barge on a canal? A caravan? YES, a caravan. I must find one at once.

The Lady of the Kennels mildly suggested that the great difficulty with a caravan was to find a suitable site where it could be parked. The usual caravan sites are nearly always in fields close to an inn or farmhouse adjoining a main road, and caravans are usually seen — in clots. I had dreamed of some solitary open glade in the woods, but, as she rightly observed, a large caravan is a cumbrous and most unwieldy thing, almost impossible to negotiate down a narrow woodland track. Also, owners of woods and private estates are prone to prohibit camping caravans in their grounds.

Difficulties always stimulate me; objections make me cussed. A caravan — a LARGE two-roomed caravan I would have, and my caravan must and SHOULD be mobile. As to the difficulty of finding the ideal parking place and then gaining the necessary permission to occupy it — why! the obvious place for it was somewhere in the Fortescue country, somewhere in Devon. On Dartmoor lived a much-beloved niece of my man's; his own home — Castle Hill — was in north Devon, near Barnstaple, and if I wanted to be on or near that wild and glorious coast there was Hartland. Some of our happiest days had been spent in the woods of Hartland Abbey, which belonged to his cousins. John had fished the little trout stream there — a brawling stream which wound through the valley until it dashed itself over the rocks in a fairy waterfall, sinking into a pool on the shore from whence it trickled down to that wonderful sea. On any of these estates I had the heart-warming certainty that I and my Blackness AND my caravan would be made welcome.

I would suggest to French H.Q. that I be allowed to canvass Devon for the A.V.F. There, bearing the proud name of Fortescue, I should be heard with more sympathy. I would go at once to London, make my proposal to the French, and find a caravan.

Where could caravans be found? Feverish enquiries ensued, until I was given the address of a firm in the north of London which supplied second-hand caravans. In an enormous shed I found no less than seventy-five, of every size and type, from the ungainly monster with a collapsible bathroom as annexe, once the property of a famous film star and her husband (I distrusted that flimsy bathroom, and feared that it might collapse when in use), to a real gypsy, horse-drawn caravan, painted gaily in green and scarlet — very fascinating; but if I bought a horse it would surely stagger soon or develop foot and mouth disease. Also, a gypsy caravan, though picturesque and romantic, has a very tiny interior, and this one needed scraping and disinfecting.

Suddenly, in a corner, I found the caravan of my dreams, a streamlined "Siddal Special." It was partitioned off into two rooms by a sliding panel inset on both sides with mirrors, and this panel also formed the door of a hanging cupboard. One entered into the kitchen end where there were a Butagaz stove with two burners and an oven, a green-enamelled sink with a hinged draining-board which could be folded over after washing up to form a shelf, a little buffet with baize-lined drawers for spoons and forks, and a lower locker for saucepans. The caravan was lined with lockers to hold stores and clothes. There was a corner cupboard for china, and even a tiny cocktail cabinet (which in my dreary day contained only a bottle of vinegar and some tumblers). Large water-containers with taps were hidden in a cupboard under the sink, and there was even A BATH — an oblong green-enamelled tank — under the floor-boards. A divan-bed with V-spring mattress (which, if necessary, could be converted into a double bed) was placed under one of the eight windows. The other end of the caravan had a small chest of drawers and a slim removable table between two other divans. So that two could live luxuriously in the caravan (each with a separate entrance), three *could* be housed, and four very uncomfortably. A lofty domed roof, surrounded with ventilators, enabled even a tall person to stand upright.

The last note of luxury was struck by the existence of an Elsan *cabinet* approached by an outside door.

Though second-hand, the caravan had hardly been occupied. Perhaps the war had interrupted some idyllic dream of life *à deux* in Arcady. All I should have to do was to substitute curtains and covers of a soft green for the beige and squashed tomato tapestry chosen by the former owners. My caravan should be placed in the woods, as was "Many Waters," and its interior decoration, like that of my Sussex cottage, must harmonise with its surroundings.

Luckily book royalties had just come in, and so another queer residence could be achieved — and *was* that very afternoon. I called it "The Ark," because it would be our refuge.

My subsequent visit to French Headquarters was equally successful, for those in command highly approved my suggestion to canvass Devon for A.V.F. I was asked to get in touch with head masters and head mistresses of schools and colleges, with Women's Institutes, Mothers' Unions, and so on, and to arrange my own detailed programme, since at that distance, lacking local railway guides and time tables, it would be almost impossible for every arrangement to be made from London. To this I readily agreed, stipulating only that they should first send me their own proposals in the form of an outline programme. And I promised to inform H.Q. directly my home on wheels was safely parked somewhere in Devon and my work about to begin. After which I lunched in a French restaurant, and then travelled back to Sussex, light of heart because at last I was able once again to do active work for France; and I had a safe home for my Blackness.

How I longed to tell *Mademoiselle* of my new plans!

CHAPTER
THIRTEEN

Gallantry

In those restless days my business with French Headquarters took me often to London, where always I was refreshed by the humour and courage of the people. I made an appointment for a hair shampoo with my old friends in New Cavendish Street, who, father and son, have tended my curls since my marriage in 1914. A bomb had shattered the glass roof of the salon, which was temporarily covered over when I arrived, but had remained open to the sky for many days. But customers, undeterred by bombs or draughty conditions, had kept all their appointments, one intrepid lady actually having a permanent wave under an umbrella while rain poured down from above. It was all taken as a great joke by the sons of the firm; and their father, though over eighty, still drove daily to the shop in a taxi, ignoring air-raid warnings and alerts, to keep an eye on the activities of his sons and give his expert advice to clients. Courageous people.

My time being short, and no bus route touching New Cavendish Street, I took a taxi once from Victoria Station, and was driven by a weary-eyed veteran with sparse grey hair. When I paid my fare I told him how much I admired the taxi-drivers of London who still carried on through the Blitz, and asked if I might be privileged to shake him by the hand. He looked surprised but pleased as he proffered a gnarled old fist, and while I searched for the fare in my capacious French bag which always contains everything except the kitchen stove, he gave me a graphic account of some of his experiences during air-raids.

"I likes to think I'm 'elpin' my grandson, so to speak, by carryin' on dahn here. 'E's in the R.A.F., 'e is, an' strafin' the Jerrys good an' proper up there." He jerked a thumb skywards. I'm a bit over age for active service — nearin' my seventy I am — but I drives people to their work or back to their 'omes in the Blitzes. As yer see, the glass of me old cab is starred a bit, but I use the lid of our dust-bin as a shield, an' then I feels like the knights of old you read of in books."

"I think you're all wonderful, both old and young," I told him. "My beloved sister lives in a Sussex village near the coast between two aerodromes, and their neighbourhood is bombed day and night. Once there were as many as forty-two unexploded bombs in and around their village. She's the head of the W.V.S. down there, and does all those outside jobs as well as running her house without a maid. Her husband, a colonel invalided out of the Indian Army and almost always in pain, is Head Air Raid Warden and lives in a tin hat. Both their girls have been serving since the outbreak of war, and the younger is now in Portsmouth; her bed was machine-gunned the other night, and once she was blown across the shelter by blast. When the Huns are over Portsmouth her mother and father can see the red glow of the fires from their garden, and wonder if their precious baby is alive or dead. It is all very fine and makes one proud to be English."

"It is that," agreed the old man, "but it makes it easier to bear ef yer doin' somethin' to 'elp; even ef it's only drivin' an old taxi. Still, I don't say but what it wouldn't be nice sometimes to get a bit of sleep."

Every one was living in an atmosphere of perpetual strain, always coping with strange emergencies. My brother's rambling old Rectory was filled with evacuees from London; the dining-room had been converted into a dormitory where three of his girls and two evacuee maidens parked slept in a row. The baby, and her nanny, who also acted as cook-general, curate, and friend, slept in another ground-floor room. Their cellars had become air-raid shelters for the children of the village school near by. A few days before I visited them they had been startled by a tremendous noise. The brakes of an army lorry carrying a gigantic gun had suddenly given way on a steep incline opposite the Rectory, and both lorry and gun had crashed through their garden wall, entered the hen-yard and crushed the hen-houses to pulp. Luckily the hens were taking their walks abroad so were not squashed, as were their precious eggs, and fortunately the invading lorry just shaved the rabbit hutches wherein were housed the children's beloved rabbits. By God's mercy the children themselves who, when at home, were nearly always to be found in that corner tending their birds and beasts, were at school when this accident happened. Mercifully no one was killed, but my brother and his wife then had to deal with the soldiers manning the lorry and gun. They were laid out on the drawing-room floor, treated for shock, bandaged in some cases, then fed and bedded down. After which, quite exhausted, the household retired — as they hoped — to rest; but at three a.m. a relief party pealed the front door bell and had to be admitted. They had had nothing to eat, and were starving. My sister-in-law, in dressing-gown, with her long fair hair in plaits, ministered to their needs, regretting sadly those pulped eggs in the hen-yard as she opened yet another precious reserve tin from her depleted store-cupboard. So ended — and began — another day.

Every one that I knew or loved was living in deadly danger at that moment. Little "Tiny," the miniature nurse who had cared for my John in France so tenderly to the end, was now matron of an emergency hospital in one of the most dangerous areas just outside London. One night she kicked no less than eleven incendiary bombs from out a ward of wounded soldiers. All night long ambulances drove up filled with civilian wounded, and she went out under a hail of bombs to receive them. She described to me the difficulty of doing this in darkness, and of treating the cases afterwards in wards and theatre lit only by a dim blue light. One incident made me laugh. Long before the war a rich man, foreseeing war ahead of him, built a luxurious underground house fitted with every comfort. Unfortunately for him, when he had come up to breathe the outer air and watch the progress of the raid, a torpedo bomb fell alongside his underground refuge, penetrated deep into the ground, exploded, and telescoped it. He was slightly wounded in the leg but very badly shocked, and was brought to Tiny's hospital in an ambulance. When she first saw him he was clinging to a bar in the roof of it like a monkey, and wouldn't — at that moment couldn't — let go, though complaining loudly of the pain in his leg, and suggesting that someone should do something about it quickly. Tiny reasoned, pleaded, and finally commanded him to let go his hold of that rail, saying that the ambulance was needed elsewhere immediately. But still he held on. At last she said:

"Listen: let go that rail at once and I will deal with your leg and put you out of pain. I assure you that you can have perfect confidence in me."

The man looked at her and snarled sarcastically:

"Never had faith in any woman yet. Not starting now." Whereupon Tiny's infectious laugh chuckled in the darkness. The man began to laugh, and at once the nervous tension was relieved, he loosed his grip and she hustled him out of the ambulance into the hospital. Her sense of humour had saved him.

All my loved ones were in danger, and for some queer reason it consoled me enormously to be living in a fighting area, and therefore sharing it. The English people were standing up to it with their native stoicism and humour. Until the Germans attempted to destroy Buckingham Palace where the King and Queen were in residence, and a bomb actually fell in the courtyard, the people looked upon all the ghastly things that were happening to them as just the chances of war — after all, *we* were doing our best to smash up Germany. But when the Huns attempted to kill their King and Queen, the English became nasty. I saw a rather horrible example of this when returning to "Many Waters" from a neighbouring town. As we entered our village street we saw ahead of us a crowd of cars and people and two or three fire-engines. I stopped the car and asked a yokel if the King or the Commander-in-Chief of our armies was honouring the village with a visit. The man was slavering with excitement, and had a horrible look in his eye as he said:

"One of our Spitfires has shot down a German plane in that field over there. You come and 'ave a look, mum; there's a lot er blood an' the pilot's 'owlin' 'orrible."

He laughed in a terrible way, spat on his hands, and then rubbed them down his corduroy trousers while he executed a kind of triumphant grotesque hopping dance of joy.

I felt as sick as poor little Kitty looked. Of course she was thinking of her boy in his bomber. I drove quickly on, and when we reached the precipice the wife of one of the gardeners congratulated me upon being absent when that same pursuing Spitfire, flying low, machine-gunned the great beech tree which flanked my garage. She showed me the ripped bark and the mass of bullet-holes (at head level) in its trunk.

"Lucky you and your little Grey Pigeon wasn't there at the time, your ladyship," she remarked.

I was thankful when the letter came from French Headquarters enclosing their proposals. It was suggested that I should first give talks to schools in Okehampton, Newton Abbot and to various Women's Institutes in the surrounding villages on the edge of Dartmoor. John's special niece was living with her husband in Manaton, and knowing that she would find the ideal site for "The Ark," I had it sent down ahead of me.

Not only is John's niece a beloved, but she combines practicality with great heart and gallantry. It would be lovely to be near her, and although she was running the Land Army with her usual energy and efficiency, she would help me out of any crisis.

"The Ark" suffered a bit on its long drive from London. Briars and branches of narrow Devonshire lanes scratched its paint, and collision with an outcrop of rock stove in the outer skin of a side panel. But this was repaired next day by the father of a family blitzed out of Plymouth, who had been taken in by John's niece and earned their keep by working in any capacity within and around the house.

Later there came a telegram from the Lady of the Kennels. She was now out of a job and rather bored. She asked if she might come down for a caravan holiday with me while looking for other voluntary war-work. She came, and at once, to my enormous relief, took over the cooking.

Our sojourn on Dartmoor was delightful, but, alas! it was not to be for long — the position was too exposed and the winter weather too bleak for me. The climate of Exmoor and John's beloved North Devon seemed preferable, and so I wrote to John's cousin, who owned Hartland Abbey, and asked if I might park my caravan in his woods. The answer was a joyful affirmative.

We packed up and went.

CHAPTER
FOURTEEN

Hartland Heaven

My little Grey Pigeon, laden to the roof with luggage, stores and equipment, plus two human beings and one Blackness, started her flight across Devon one lovely morning of early summer. The great tors of Dartmoor, so grim and terrifying in winter and semi-darkness, their heads and shoulders seen against a background of sullen sky, were now swathed in scarves of pale blue mist. Later a fresh wind swept the vapours of the night high into a blue heaven to form great white cumulus clouds which cast deep violet shadows, now in a valley beneath, then on the summit of a tor as, driven by the wind, they sailed over the landscape. As we approached Exmoor clumps of golden gorse burned here and there amid the brown heather. Sometimes a patch of late bluebells was lit into loveliness amid a sea of bracken as though a bit of sky had been torn off by the wind and fallen to earth. We passed through sleepy little villages, the white thatched cottages of North Devon replacing the sterner stone of the little houses of Dartmoor built to withstand exposure to wilder weather at a higher altitude. Dartmoor is bleak, bracing, dramatic, magnificent, but somehow frightening. Exmoor is lovely, luxuriant, relaxing —

and cosy. Born amid the biting winds of the east coast of England, I found the air of North Devon too gentle when I first married, but after eleven years of life in the sunshine of the South of France, I should now find the warmer, softer atmosphere of Hartland very comforting.

Hartland! I could — and can — never think of that heavenly place without a feeling of bottled rapture, as though the wine of life were secretly bubbling and fermenting inside me and would burst the bottle — unless it were uncorked and the fumes of ecstasy let free. Well — soon I could uncork. And I did hope that the fumes would not distil into a rain of joyful tears when this happened.

Living so long abroad my English seasons had become muddled. Would those giant bushes of yellow azaleas, taller than my very tall John, be now in bloom bordering the approach to the Abbey, drenching the air with their indescribable sweetness? Would the steep wooded slopes be carpeted with bluebells; and the wild iris which once formed a river of gold running beside the little stream flowing through the valley to the sea, would the iris still beflag the meadows? That little stream that John had loved so much, fishing its deep brown pools for the shy trout which lurked under its banks and sunken boulders, while I paddled deliciously in its babbling, chuckling shallows lower down, or bathed beneath the waterfall which dashed over the rock cliffs to form a still lagoon on the shore, whence it finally lost itself in that beautiful dangerous sea. Would the clumps of thrift be in flower on the springy turf edging the cliffs?

How wonderfully blue the sea had looked, seen through a fringe of sea-pinks — those vivid sea-pinks that grew also in fissures of the great jagged rocks which, stretching far out into the sea, made that coast so treacherous.

Revisiting these loved haunts — without my John — must be fraught with pain as well as rapture; but that is life — as we know it here. At any rate Hartland Abbey was once more surrounded by love. For a time it had been lonely. The chain of walled gardens built by the monks of olden time, where tall lilies grew and roses rioted, and peaches, nectarines and enormous pears ripened upon the sun-baked walls, had been, perforce, neglected after the death of John's cousin who had lived there for so long. The heir, having other large estates which must be maintained, had offered Hartland Abbey and its surrounding loveliness to John and me for a ludicrously small rent, saying that the author of *The Story of a Red Deer*, a Devon man and the historian of the British Army, must not be allowed to go and live abroad!

To live in the place of our dreams . . . ! But loving it so much we could never have borne to see it gradually degenerating. In place of the army of gardeners, once employed, we could perhaps engage one and a half — a man and a boy. Even that would be an effort. Inside the Abbey, instead of a butler, an odd man and a staff of female servants we should have to manage with a married couple or a cook and a house-parlour-maid. We should have to close the upper floor and live in one wing. Even then, the huge kitchen in the cloisters beneath was half a mile from the dining-room. Ancient abbeys were not built on a labour-saving design. There would be repairs — there were endless stables and outbuildings to keep up. We must choke sentiment with sense and refuse that wonderful offer; and we did — with what heartbreak no one but ourselves ever knew.

There followed a period of emptiness for the Abbey. It was so large, taxation was crushing, labour was difficult to find, and servants do not willingly take service in a house that is twenty-six miles from the nearest town. Then the heir of Hartland gave the place to his elder son, whose young wife, also a Devonian, loved it as passionately as it deserved. During this war they could not occupy the Abbey themselves, so they let it to a Preparatory School for boys evacuated from London. The damage done by that band of boys was incalculable. All valuable carpets and precious pieces of furniture had been locked away in one room, but the Grenville portraits, inset in panels high up in the walls of the great dining-hall, were deemed to be safe. Who could have imagined that little boys would catapult such priceless paintings? The owner found his ancestors with slashed faces, and the canvas scarred and torn by stones. . . . Outside not a summer-house retained a pane of glass, and those undisciplined little hooligans had smashed their way through gardens and shrubberies as well, leaving ruin in their wake. Naturally that school had been evicted, and for the moment the Abbey was empty once more, guarded by my cousins who lived in a lodge at its gates, but the damage was done.

As we neared the gates my heart began to bump unsteadily. Should we be greeted by the squawk and screech of angry peacocks as of yore? Should we see black sheep grazing in the park?

Yes! There was one peacock perched on the battlements, another with his tail spread gorgeously in the sunshine near the entrance steps surrounded by admiring females; and the black shapes dotting the grass beyond could only be the famous black sheep.

At the sound of the approaching car a door opened and a girlish figure emerged with a burst, followed by three little girls, who all ran to meet me with a cheerful welcome.

"Peggy! You've come back to Hartland. Oh! Your ENORMOUS caravan. What a job they had to get it on the site! The young man who towed it here from Dartmoor arrived late in the evening, parked it near the Abbey and deserted us, saying that it was too dark to get it on to the site. He just leaped into the towing-car and drove off home, leaving *us* to cope! Our men were splendid next day, and thoroughly enjoyed themselves with a tractor. You should have seen old Kivell (the bailiff). He took off the gate leading from that steep lane on to the site, and *when* they got the tractor and caravan through it — this seemed to *us* impossible — he insisted upon turning the caravan round, by hand, because the door was on the weather side! Now your entrance is protected by a high bank."

She sent one of the little girls indoors to fetch the caravan keys, and while we waited told us that the Abbey had been let to the Monkey Club of London, and she had been superintending some preliminary cleaning. "Only at present I've been able to get only one woman, and it needs an army of them to clear up after that awful school," she chuckled. (I was to learn that she always chuckled through any crisis and misfortune so long as it didn't touch her beloved little family.)

"Monkey Club?" I asked, mystified.

"Yes, that famous club for perfecting young girls in art, languages, domestic science — what you will, or rather what *they* will, before the war swallows them. The motto of the club is — 'See no evil. Hear no evil. Speak no evil' — *you* know, the Three Wise Monkeys."

"Ohhh!" I said. It sounded very intriguing.

"Here are your keys. You go on ahead, and we'll follow and see if we can be useful. Children! Catch your ponies and you can ride up."

We drove on through the park, The Blackness with his head out of a window, his nose twitching ecstatically as he scented a very heaven of rabbits. After a struggle with the park gate we found ourselves at the foot of a typical Devon lane, like a narrow green tunnel, with high banks overgrown with ferns, honeysuckle and brambles, the hedgerows on their summits almost forming an arch. It climbed steeply up a tor, and half-way up on the left was a broken-down gate, its many pieces interlocked. This was the entrance to the caravan site, and there, sure enough, stood my monstrous "Ark," moored in an open space of rough grass under two wild cherry trees.

Even my little Grey Pigeon had the greatest difficulty in entering that place. The approach was so steep and the lane so narrow that to this day I cannot imagine how those men manoeuvred that enormous caravan on to the site, and I was filled with cowardly thankfulness that this had been done before my arrival. But once there, its position could not have been more perfect — half-way up a great tor, in a clearing of the woods, facing south, with a wonderful view across the valley to the great beacon tower of St. Nectan's Church, which rose majestically from a sea of foliage, a landmark for sailors. Through bird song and the music of little hidden streams and pixie wells boomed the distant roar of Atlantic rollers as they crashed against great rocks. The tide was coming in. Overhead hawks soared and swooped. As in the past, every variety of hawk and owl were to be found in Hartland, every variety of scent — honeysuckle, hot bracken, moss, fungi, leaf mould, resin, wild flowers, dominated by the smell of the sea.

We unlocked the caravan, and The Blackness immediately flew inside and made a tour of investigation to see if his home on wheels was still intact. Satisfied on this point, he rudely jostled his way out again and rushed off into the bracken on hunting bent, while we unpacked the car and made ourselves cosy. The children were thrilled by the caravan, and peered longingly inside, but they were adorable children, trained by wise parents to be natural and forthcoming, but never uppish, precocious or unruly. Actually they obeyed instantly every injunction of their mother. Yet they were delightfully full of fun and devil.

"Come along home now, children," commanded their mother. "I'm sure Cousin Peggy will let you explore the caravan another day. She's tired now and has got to get it tidy and straight before it's dark. By the way, Peggy, I'm afraid the pump of your well doesn't work. It shall be seen to as soon as we can get a man. I'll take the children home, and then drive up later in the car with some cans of our drinking water."

We were to find that the pump was a temperamental pump. Sometimes it worked and sometimes it went on strike. We were afterwards informed by old "Grand-Dad," an ancient of the village, whose grand-daughter came daily to work for us while he fetched water from the well and cut the grass and bracken on the site, that it had been bought second-hand, and the pipe that fed it was only "on loan" and reclaimed from time to time by the owner, who was the man who *should* repair the pump. This sounded sinister, for what is life in a caravan or a tent without water? Had I not been a cousin by marriage of the owner of the Abbey, and borne the name of Fortescue, those repairs, perhaps, had never been done. As it was I was sacrosanct, though referred to by old Kivell when talking of me to his mistress as, "'Er up over."

Oh, the lovely peace of that first night in Hartland! To lie in one's bunk and stare across dim woods to the noble tower of St. Nectan's black against a starlit sky, hearing only the cries of owls and the sleepy sob of the sea.

The Blackness, tired out by travelling and the excitement of the chase, lay curled up on the opposite berth, having decided — to my relief — that my bunk was too narrow for us both. In her room on the other side of the partition wall slumbered my companion, wearied by practical deeds. She had fixed up the new cylinder of the Butagaz, tucked up the little Grey Pigeon in rugs for the night (for she must sleep in the open behind the caravan), arranged her kitchen to her liking, and now was sleeping the sleep of one wearied by well-doing.

What a fantastic kaleidoscope is life. Little did I dream when staying in the sheltered luxury of the Abbey with my John in 1914 that I should come back without him twenty-seven years later and live in a caravan in the woods with a war acquaintance and a little black dog.

But surely — surely — he was somewhere near. Surely he would plead to leave — even Heaven — to share the rapture of Hartland with me?

CHAPTER
FIFTEEN

The Abbey

The Blackness and I woke early and simultaneously as the first rays of the sun, filtering through the trees, cast a shifting pattern of light and shadow into the green interior of "The Ark." He had fallen asleep before I did, and I had lovingly watched the twitching of that black nose and the intermittent stiffening and kick of feathered legs as I listened to his tiny muffled barks in his sleep. He was doubtless rushing madly in chase of rabbits in the Hunters' Heaven — which would be — Hartland. What happiness it gave me as I watched and listened to know that he would wake to find reality perhaps even better than his dream! Now he was awake, and already braced himself for action. Upright, on stiff hind legs, he peered out from his eastern window at the dawn, then, with a swift turn of the head, rolled an anxious eye in my direction and, seeing that I too was awake, leaped to the floor, then upon my chest and stared eagerly into my eyes. In his I saw two blazing question marks, and after we had exchanged a swift embrace I got up and quietly opened the door. Here were no red terrors. Here he could run free. With one bound he leaped forth, fled towards the woods and vanished into the ferns.

Life! Liberty! Ecstasy! HARTLAND!

We had been very quiet, so quiet that we had not disturbed the sleeper next door. I crept back into my bunk and relaxed.

It was an exciting day for us all. First we must organise our caravan life, visit the farm and ensure a supply of milk from the Guernsey cows (luckily I was classed as a member of the family, and could buy the surplus, which was not enough to be worth precious petrol to take it sixteen miles to the nearest town). I must visit the gardens, order vegetables and fruit, and arrange for their transport. Then I must interview the village maiden proposed by my cousins as helper, and her grandfather who would cut the grass and fern around the caravan, and haul up water from our well some way down the side of the tor. That done, there was still time to walk through the meadows bordering the little stream down to the sea, where The Blackness nearly gave us heart attacks by his mountaineering activities on the edge of those dangerous rock cliffs.

Approaching it through peaceful meadows or the stillness of the woods, that stretch of sea always gives one a dramatic shock. Even on calm days, as the tide comes in, great rollers curl and break over the rocks, one hears the snarl of the undertow with each retreating wave and, knowing the strength of those treacherous currents which swirl around the coast of North Devon, a little shiver always runs down my spine. The sea has a tremendous fascination for me, but I am terrified of it all the same. I have the same feeling for snow peaks and glaciers, knowing the mighty force of sudden mountain storms and the danger of avalanches and bewildering blizzards which in half an hour can obliterate every familiar landmark. They excite and exhilarate, but fill me with a very fearful joy.

On the cliffs a few tufts of thrift still bloomed pink against the background of green and blue sea, and as we wandered back along the woodland path we found the steep slopes on either side of us misted with bluebells. Already they had lost their first dazzling blue, but now formed a tender blue-grey background for thousands of rose-pink campions, lit magically by the sun shining through their petals as its rays filtered here and there through the over-arching trees.

We decided to have our luncheon and then go down to the Abbey to see if we could help to get it straight for those Wise Monkeys who would soon be scampering all over it.

Inside the Abbey we found dust and dereliction. The entrance hall was bare, the long corridor which used to be almost a picture gallery, with bare walls and floor. In the great dining-room we found one lady, solitary and sad, throned in a carved chair regarding the chaos before her — chairs piled upon a table, dust and straw everywhere. She turned her head and regarded us through dark-rimmed spectacles like a deeply shocked owl.

"If seven maids with seven mops swept it for half a year . . ." I quoted the query cheerfully.

"Even then I doubt if they could get it clear," she snapped in sepulchral tones.

This was one of the two directresses of the Club of the Three Wise Monkeys. Having moved the club from London to various places in Devon, from which war conditions and calamities had evicted them, they had learned the temperament of the Devonians — so like that of the Provençaux — everything would be done *"Demain — ou après-demain"* — and *never* unless some strong-willed and patient person pushed behind — and continued to push until something was accomplished. So the two partners had arrived a week early to do the pushing. The creator of the Monkey Club we found with her head tied up in a duster, sweeping clouds of dust down the back stairs with the energy and determination which are two of her chief characteristics. It is altogether admirable when a master mind such as hers can bend itself to the creation of order from chaos, and does not disdain even the most menial tasks personally to achieve it. Later I was to find out that this extraordinary woman could not only lecture on the history and literature of every country in the world, racing through the centuries, never forgetting a date or a period, quoting from poets, philosophers and historians, but positively enjoyed higher mathematics, finding the solving of intricate problems a fascinating pastime, just as she enjoyed the concoction and cooking of elaborate dishes, which she made like a chef.

The inferiority complex this super-woman gave me was almost cancelled by her warm and loving interest in all I thought and did. Her great heart, already so full of her "girls" and their work, interests and future careers, yet had room for mine, and her sympathy and enthusiasm encouraged me at a very dark moment.

But all this I was to experience later. When I first

saw her she was a veritable Goddess of the Broom, enveloped in clouds of dust through which I could only dimly realise the most forceful of her characteristics.

My cousin's voice echoed down the corridor:

"Peggy! *Can* that be you? Angel, to come as you promised. I'm in the library. . . ."

The library! The loveliest room in the Abbey, as I remembered it. Book-lined from floor to ceiling, softly carpeted, overlooking that wonderfully peaceful view — the Deer Park, the black sheep grazing, peacocks sunning themselves in the foreground and, beyond, the Happy Valley — bordered by the little trout stream and climbing woods, above which reared the majestic tower of St. Nectan's.

Wandering home in the old days after a long day of fishing, paddling and bathing, what a welcome those glowing lamps in the library gave one as one approached the Abbey, and what a sybaritic joy it was after such a day to sink into those deep armchairs and revel in the luxury of a real Devonshire tea, with bowls of thick golden cream, cut-rounds, saffron and every sort of cake, perhaps fat early strawberries. Flowers everywhere — lilies, roses, violets, azaleas, lilies of the valley in their season; the firelight gleaming on the polished silver tea service, and the white hair of our hostess — aunt (by marriage) of the present owner of the Abbey — whose cooing voice, so like that of a wood pigeon, pressed one to burst buttons already stretched nearly to that point by the fat and plentiful fare she provided for her guests.

Now I found that lovely room still gracious, but dusty and encumbered with furniture and family portraits whose faces my cousin was irreverently flicking with a duster.

"Poor old things — they've been shut up so long. Now that those boys have gone I'm going to hang 'em up wherever I can find a nail. Those old Shakespearian prints, too. Could you hang them in one of the bedrooms, preferably where the wall-paper is torn or faded? The whole Abbey ought to be done up, but who can do anything in war-time? Thank Heaven you've turned up, because no one else has — my *one* charwoman has failed me AND the two directors of the Monkey Club have turned up a week early" — here her usual fat chuckle. "We warned them they'll be fearfully uncomfortable — they might have been less so if they'd come on the appointed day — but then again they might *not*. We live in Devon, and now it's Devon in war-time." She chuckled out a groan.

"Anyway, the head of the club is doing the work of the army of charwomen you promised her," I said. "Through clouds of glorious dust I saw her dealing with the back staircase." Then I and my companion climbed the front stairs to hang the Shakespearian prints while The Blackness and my cousin's little lady dog ran marathon races down the corridors.

The Abbey was not nearly straight when hordes of Monkeys arrived in taxis, followed by a lorry of luggage. Some of them were taking a course of Domestic Science, and were able to practise it at once. Led by their chief, who had miraculously found local women to scrub and clean while the staff of the club (from London) arranged bedrooms, dining-room, pantries and kitchen, the members proceeded to fit up studies and lecture-room, finding it great fun. They were enchanted by the Abbey and its lovely surroundings, and those who possessed horses were madly excited when told that they could have them sent down to Hartland. The beauty of the place so went to the head of the artistic young lady who was to coach members in painting and design, that she went to the village and bought a large pot of sky-blue paint, with which she was inspired to paint skirting, window frames and seats in privy places of what was once the nursery wing. Everywhere there was an atmosphere of vital activity and excitement. When walking through the woods down to the sea we would be passed by lovely damsels wearing swimming suits and riding bicycles. Monkeys swarmed in the shrubberies and climbed the cliffs. The Abbey lawns were strewn with sun bathers, and some of the members rolled out the tennis court and marked it for play. We always knew when the hours of very intense study were over and the members were free to roam where they pleased by the scream of enraged peacocks as Monkeys burst forth from every door of the Abbey and disturbed their vainglorious peace. Hartland was now very much awake.

I did not at first see very much of the inhabitants of the Abbey, for I was inundated with requests from schools, colleges, women's institutes, mothers' unions and rotary clubs to give them talks about France and the spirit of resistance of the French people. I had to plan my programme and consult maps to ascertain distances, for I was to cover the whole of Devon by road. Devonshire is a very uncomfortable place to tour, and though not a very enormous county, the two great moors — Exmoor and Dartmoor — split it into two, and must be skirted to reach the important towns, so that it would never be possible to give more than one — at most two — talks a day if I were to return to the caravan at night, and to get anywhere at all I must first drive to Bideford, sixteen miles from Hartland, before I began my real journey. The obvious thing to do was to fulfil all the engagements in towns and villages as far as Exeter and Okehampton, then concentrate on South Devon, where I might possibly be obliged to stay nights in hotels, leaving my Blackness in the charge of his devoted aunt. Directly posters were put up announcing my forthcoming talks, offers of hospitality were showered upon me by warm-hearted friends or strangers from that particular locality. Would I lunch with them before my lecture — or have tea afterwards? Better still, would I stay the night, for this would enable my hostess to invite some friends who were longing to meet me, for dinner. In nearly every case I refused. I am sure that I must have seemed very ungracious and unsociable, for it was impossible to make people believe in the agony of nervousness I always suffer before I speak, and my complete exhaustion after my efforts on a public platform to soften the hearts of the unsympathetic, and turn them from hostility and misunderstanding to active sympathy. I knew that I should prove but a deadly dreary guest, absent-minded and crumbling bread pills at a preceding luncheon, and sapped and yawning at night when the ordeal was over. Not even the stimulus of good wine could animate, for alcohol poisons me and makes my neck ache (so maddening to live in a country of vines, make my own good wine and be unable to drink it!). So that it was really considerate of me to refuse those kind invitations.

My first important date was to speak to four hundred girls in a college in Bideford. The headmistress, a lover of dogs, pressed me to bring The Blackness with me, as all the girls longed to make the acquaintance of the hero of *Trampled Lilies* (I had thought that I had made *the French* the subject of my book, but The Blackness, so important a factor in my life, intruded — as he always will!). When I told her that Dominie was, alas, intensely nervous of people — especially children, for those in the Midi had teased and tormented him if they got a chance — and of all noises, since his war experiences, she pleaded:

"Oh, Lady Fortescue, do, DO bring him! The girls will be *so* disappointed if you don't."

I agreed, with the warning that I could not guarantee his good behaviour, and that if I brought him he might possibly wreck our afternoon. She was willing to take the risk, and so on the day appointed Dominie and I set forth for Bideford.

With much apprehension in my heart I was towed on to that platform by The Blackness. His appearance was greeted by a storm of applause (I realised that it was all for HIM), and I fully expected him to go mad with fright, entangle his lead in the legs of the speaker's table, probably upset the traditional tumbler of water and, perhaps, me. To my complete amazement he seemed to LIKE it! This was a friendly noise, a welcoming noise, an admiring noise, HIS noise — all for him. He regarded his audience with head on one side and bright smiling eyes, and then began to waggle with pleasure, little dancing steps, and his little round stern with its flickering apology for a tail, turning almost to meet his head with the endearing squirm common to happy spaniels. The applause, of course, increased, but so did his gyrations. The headmistress by my side suggested:

"Won't you put him up on the table so that the girls at the back of the hall can see him?"

Nervously I tried the experiment, and he was then greeted by rousing cheers from four hundred young and lusty throats. This, I thought, would be the end. But no! Dominie acknowledged the cheers by loud and joyful barks. His first appearance upon a public platform had been a triumphant success, after which I feared that my coming performance must be an anti-climax. His behaviour that day was exemplary. I lifted him from the table and placed him upon his own little rug by my feet, where he instantly curled up and composed himself for sleep, only waking up to poke me behind my knees with an impatient nose when he considered that I had talked long enough.

Those girls were a lovely audience. When I speak I never use notes, because for me it means putting on spectacles to read them, and taking them off again to enable me to see my audience. I found that this restless business made me nervous, and in those split seconds lost me the attention of my audience. It was better just to speak from my heart and blather on, even though I might forget important points I had meant to emphasise. On that occasion the fresh eager faces below and before me soon made me forget my nervousness. This was a non-critical audience that longed to hear all about poor France, unlike many of those I was destined to face later, whose hostility towards the ally who had "let us down" had to be transformed into warm sympathy. On one occasion there was a woman sitting in the front row of my audience with an expression as sour as a lemon and a mouth set like a spring trap. I was opening my mouth to speak when I caught her baleful eye, and instead of the opening sentence I should have uttered I found myself pleading with her to change her expression.

"Madame! PLEASE don't look at me like that! If you do, I can't speak. You hate France because you don't know what really happened to her. I lived in France for eleven years, and worked with and for the French Army till Dunkirk. If you'll just change that expression on your face I'll explain the tragedy of France — and I'll make you cry."

I *did* make her cry, and at the end of my talk she gave me a big subscription for General de Gaulle's *Volontaires*, and became a loyal member of A.V.F. The English are a hard-headed but a just and generous people.

My audience of girls was quite different. They sat, tense and thrilled, particularly by stories of the courage of the French children, stories which were brought to French H.Q. in London by members of the Underground Movement, typed in cellars on odd slips of paper, or told us by word of mouth. They particularly loved the tale of the children forced to learn the goose-step and German doctrines in a Vichy school on pain of whipping. Their mothers had been bribed to send their children to this school by the promise of one good solid meal for them at midday. In a starving country few mothers could resist such a bribe. One day a very smart German officer drove up to inspect the school. He left his glittering car outside. The children were having their so-called recreation, practising (no doubt in a spirit of mockery) the strutting goose-step. The moment the German officer disappeared into the school they fell upon his car — and wrecked its loveliness. With flints they scratched the V sign deep into its enamelled panels, and with pocket knives they slashed V's in the leather upholstery inside; with mud and spittle they smeared V's on all the windows and the windscreen. And those children had been warned that they'd be whipped within an inch of their lives if they didn't learn the goose-step . . . !

The little daughter of Madame Cathala, head of the Resistance in Toulouse, was travelling in a tram with her elder sister. A German officer got in and sat down on her other side. The child regarded him with scornful disgust, then turned to her sister and said:

"*Annette! Si je pouvais changer ma place. Il y a une mauvaise odeur à côte de moi!*"

Not bad for eight years old. How the girls laughed and clapped! When I finished speaking there was such a lovely noise, MY noise this time, that I rolled an eye at the ceiling to see if it was cracking. Then, The Blackness and I, having "taken our call" together, the headmistress suggested a cup of tea in her room. As we walked down the corridor we met a procession of four hundred girls each carrying the chair she had occupied while I was speaking, and as each child passed us she bent with her burden to pat Dominie. Any unusual object generally scared him stiff, and he particularly objected to being caressed by strangers. But to-day the vision of a girl crowned with a chair or holding one in front of her seemed to have no terrors for him, and he quietly accepted their homage before being crammed with cakes in the parlour. When we had nearly finished tea there came a timid knock at the door. Two little maidens stood there holding — autograph books. Behind them I saw an unending line of girls the whole length of the corridor — all holding autograph books or slips of paper! The head mistress looked at me apologetically.

"Oh dear, I ought to have anticipated this," she began, but seeing my smile and outstretched hand, she continued: "Oh, it *is* good of you — are you *sure* you're not too tired?"

I signed all those books and slips of paper, and I must admit that I *was* tired at the end, but how could I resist those dear girls! They all enrolled as members of A.V.F. that afternoon, and brought me besides a school hat filled with money they had collected among themselves for de Gaulle's *Volontaires*. Later I became the proud *Marraine* of those girls, and possess the college badge presented to me at the time of my adoption.

When I got back to the cosy hotel where I had decided to stay the night to enable me to fulfil two more engagements not very far from Bideford next day, I was accosted in the hall by the manageress.

"A suitcase has been left here for you, Lady Fortescue."

"A *suitcase*? There must be some mistake."

"Oh no! It's addressed to you, and was brought here by a band of young ladies from the college, who asked me to take great care of it till you came back."

I opened it in my room and found — what do you think? MORE autograph albums, from the day-girls of the college who had gone home at noon for their weekly half-holiday and so had missed my lecture! Leaving Bideford next day, which anyhow would be quite full up with work, rather than disappoint those children I tackled those albums at once, and a very long job it was. I had frog's hands after so much writing.

The next day I had to address a huge audience — a boys' school and a girls' school combined. A large cinema had been taken for the occasion, and though nearly blinded by a spot-light aimed from a high gallery (which must have made my face, unadorned by heavy stage make-up, look like bad beef), dimly I saw large senior boys and girls, middle-sized boys and girls and, in front, kindergarten boys and girls. How to hold the attention of the small boys and girls while I told stories of the *Volontaires* which would hold the attention of the seniors? And vice versa? However, it had to be done, and somehow I did it. At the end, when the senior boy proposed three cheers for the speaker, I descended from the platform and was startled by loud strains of martial music. One of the boys had climbed into the gallery and was manipulating the theatre organ. Never before had I marched alone to the accompaniment of a military march, but the fact that it was a French march played in honour of France told me that my appeal had had its effect. Afterwards, the head master of the boys' school told me that to the deep chagrin of that amateur organist he could not find a copy of the Marseillaise with which to play me out.

There was a terrifying mass meeting of women's institutes to address in Exeter Town Hall. We had persuaded Lady Fortescue (*Madame la Comtesse*), as wife of the Lord Lieutenant of Devon (my nephew by marriage and exactly my age, for my John married late and was the ninth of a family of fourteen), to be President of A.V.F. for Devon. She was to take the chair on this occasion, so that I was sure of at least one kindred spirit to support me. Having refused all invitations to lunch before the ordeal, I crept into a little café and toyed with some vegetarian mess, drank some wishy-washy coffee and smoked nervous cigarettes until the moment came to walk to the Town Hall and go through my ordeal. Town halls are generally dark and depressing inside, and this one was no exception. As instructed, I entered the back door behind and below the stage. A long stone corridor, which seemed to be deserted, faced me, but suddenly from the embrasure of a window a slender figure shot forth and fell upon me. It was my niece, Madame la Comtesse.

"Oh, Peggy darling, here you are! I've been hiding here till you came. I simply didn't dare go up on that terrifying platform alone. All those women would have been so disappointed. They're expecting a talk from Lady Fortescue, the writer, and if I'd appeared before you did they'd have had such a shock and would have said to themselves:

"'Oh, it's *that* Lady Fortescue — we're always seeing and hearing *her* — you know, Red Cross and prisoners of war stuff.'"

"And I had made up my mind that if *I* arrived first I'd hide in a corner till you came, lest I disappoint the women for not being 'The Countess,'" I confessed.

We were always being mixed up. I was continually being praised and congratulated for my (her) good work in the county, and she being thanked for her (my) books.

On this occasion the two trembling Lady Fortescues crawled up the steps at the back of the platform and made their appearance together at the appointed hour, where Madame la Comtesse duly introduced the speaker. I was almost paralysed to find that I must stand in the centre of a half-moon of presidents of W.I.'s from the whole of North Devon, but I strove to forget them and to see only the rosy faces of the Devon women in the audience.

When I was on the stage in my youth I once asked Jimmy Welch, the comedian who played the leading part in *When Knights Were Bold* for thousands of performances, if he did not get utterly sick of saying and doing the same thing over and over again. He replied:

"No, never. It is like salmon fishing. You try different flies for the same fish, and every fish plays you up in a different way. Audiences are like that."

I found out the truth of this. My Devon audiences of country women couldn't have been more cosy. Constantly they broke into my speeches, and their

"Oh's" and "Ah's" and "Who'd have thought it?" were sympathetic interjections which, when I had got used to them, could only assure me of the interest of my audience. Nowhere but in Devon did my audiences, so to speak, join in the conversation.

As public speaking, even to cosy audiences, is always exhausting, I tried when I could to space an interval of two, perhaps three, days between engagements, and to spend my holidays in Hartland. And I was anxious to know more of the inmates of the Abbey.

CHAPTER
SIXTEEN

Monkey Tricks

In the intervals between lectures I had as many opportunities as I cared to take of understanding the ideals of the Club of the Three Wise Monkeys and of soaking in its atmosphere. I soon learned to speak of the girls as "the members"; terms were sessions and the instructors professors or coaches. It was in no sense a school or college, but a CLUB. The members made their own rules, and the founder of the club was always invited to attend all conferences or committees, where naturally she could have vetoed any rules or plans. But it was never necessary for her to exercise this power because, with her tact and understanding, she always succeeded in putting her case (when she frankly disapproved of a plan) in such a sane and reasonable way, her questions often faintly tinged with kindly irony, that always the project appeared undesirable or, if put into practice, would seem faintly ridiculous. Modern girls are very intelligent and sensitive. Once the pros and cons of a thing are put before them they almost inevitably make the right decision. Their founder played upon their young enthusiasm, inspired them unconsciously with high ideals and stimulated their imaginations. She could do everything in the world (except darn stockings) so much better than anyone else. Her learning was so vast and her sense of humour so keen that her judgment had tremendous weight. Any member could approach her or her partner at any hour of the day and be sure of the sympathy and help of those two over-worked women. There was nothing aloof or Olympian in their attitude, and the moment one entered the Abbey one sensed the throbbing vitality and happiness of its atmosphere. It was a proud day for me when I was proposed as an honorary life member of the club and when *every* member seconded this proposal.

I started giving coffee parties in my caravan, inviting six or seven Monkeys at a time, and the girls loved the informality of those summer evenings as much as I did. They paid me the great compliment of treating me as a contemporary, as did also the founder, coaches, and professors, so that I always heard both sides of every problem or situation, sometimes very amusing, but also a somewhat delicate position demanding reticence and tact.

The Blackness was an abominable host. He hated those sociable evenings, and the moment he saw the head of the first Monkey appearing above the bracken he began to roar. No overtures would placate him; greedy as he was he refused even biscuits from the hands of my guests. Flumping himself in the most remote corner of the caravan he sulked in solitude, only rousing himself when they made their farewells. Before they were out of sight he sprang from the caravan, tore up a fern or a trailing spray of honeysuckle, and then did mad tearums round me and the caravan, with his bit of greenery half choking joyful barks which said: "At LAST they've gone! NOW we are alone together again and the fun begins!"

"Your dog is VERY rude!" the Monkeys called back to me the first time he disgraced my hospitality.

"He is — *abominably*," I agreed.

The only friends he made in the Monkey Club were the founder, a great dog-lover who stuffed him dangerously when we went to the Abbey for tea, and a gentle and very brilliant little Jewish refugee — a qualified doctor — who coached languages. She and Dominie understood and loved each other at sight. She tickled his heart out of him and whispered secrets in his ear. I could always leave him with "Doc," as every one called her, and know him to be perfectly happy, and she, often bitterly lonely with tragic memories of her home and family, found comfort in his silent but always sympathetic companionship.

Life at Hartland, though completely sheltered from the dangers of the war, was yet eventful, interesting, and sometimes amusing. The founder of the Monkey Club liked to keep its members always on tiptoe. Neither the professors nor the girls ever knew what next would be asked of them. Suddenly the servants of the Abbey would all be given leave of absence for the whole day and the Monkeys would be asked to replace them. The domestic science students must swiftly plan and prepare meals, knowing that these would be eaten and every dish criticised by their founder, who was something of a *gourmet* (*not gourmand*). Junior members must transform themselves into kitchen-maids and scullery maids, and members not taking the domestic science course must become temporary parlour-maids. Perhaps after dinner, when washing up was finished, an impromptu entertainment would be organised. Members might invite friends from outside, and must be clad in evening dress to act as hostesses. Dances were often planned, and the domestic science students provided the most delicious refreshments, so that work was always an ingredient of pleasure.

One delightful dinner followed by a fancy dress dance was organised to celebrate my birthday. No one was allowed to spend anything on her dress, which had to be improvised from anything that could be found in the wardrobe — or the Abbey. The members insisted that I should wear some fancy costume, and I racked my brain to think of something suitable to my years and grey curls. In the end I took a white sheet and with a pot of scarlet enamel painted the Cross of Lorraine from hem to hem on the section that I should drape from neck to toe, and I made a great sword of cardboard which I painted on both sides with silver aluminium paint. Dominie had been taken for a walk in the wet woods — of course it was raining hard on the great day — so that I could be left in peace to complete my costume. He returned at the end of the afternoon when my dress was spread out on the camp bed to allow the paint to dry, and his companion, obeying his frantic barks for admittance to me, unthinkingly opened the door to admit him. With one bound a ball of black ecstasy leaped on to the bed, dancing with muddy feet on the white sheet and leaving muddy paw-marks all around the *Croix de Lorraine* which I had taken so much pains to draw and paint. In one minute the work of hours was ruined! OH . . . ! There was no time to organise another dress. I had intended to represent Fighting France — *La France Combattante* — but now I was too disheartened to think of anything else, and so I sent a message down to the Abbey to explain to the members why I must appear as myself. Their reply was: "No fancy dress, no admittance — and it's YOUR party." In despair I thought of painting over those dear but destructive footmarks with white distemper. At first that had an even worse effect — grey splodges all down what would be the front, but they eventually dried and faintly camouflaged the marks. Well! that would have to do. I wound the sheet tightly around my body, and draped one end over my left shoulder to form a swinging cape. Then I bound a scarlet silk sash around my head to represent a *Bonnet rouge* and shod myself with scarlet mules. Thus, with uplifted sword in hand, I led the procession of masqueraders around the great dining-hall of the Abbey, and was unanimously awarded the first prize, which I ceded to three of the junior members who sat cross-legged in a row on a table dressed in buff Jaegar vests and pants (their ski-ing underwear) with tails of plaited wool and buff skull caps, one shielding her eyes with her hands, the second covering her ears, and the third her mouth — the badge of the club, the Three Wise Monkeys.

They were wonderful, and it was quite difficult to select the winners, for all dresses were original and most ingenious. At dinner, in mercy, I cut the string of one girl disguised as a parcel so that she might breathe and eat, and removed a saucepan from the head of another who represented domestic science and was hung with onions, carrots, turnips, wooden spoons, a nutmeg grater and so forth.

We had an uproarious evening, crowned with happiness for me when the founder of the club presented me with a bowl filled with money collected from entrance and dinner tickets, hoop-la fees, etc., as the clubs contribution to help the Fighting French. With her understanding heart she knew that I should appreciate this more than any other birthday present they could give me. In farewell I stood before Mademoiselle X, the French professor, a sad and loyal Bretonne, and silently pointed my silver sword towards the stars. Her eyes filled with tears. She understood that victorious gesture and gently inclined her head.

During the mornings and evenings the Monkeys studied furiously their special subjects, working with private coaches in small classes, or reading alone. All of them had to pass very stiff examinations to gain diplomas. Monkeys of earlier years were already holding important posts, the good linguists and secretaries in the Ministry of Information or the Foreign Office, the domestic science students in the Ministry of Food, some of them giving cookery demonstrations to huge audiences all over the country.

In the afternoons of summer in Hartland the members were turned loose, and drifted out of doors. Some of them now kept their horses at the Abbey, the Lord of the Manor, himself a keen horseman, giving them stabling, pasture and every facility. Others hired hard-mouthed hacks in the village, and once one of these bolted with its long-legged rider and headed straight for those dangerous cliffs. Unable to stop her horse, the intrepid Monkey astride him kept her head. As they rocketed past a spreading tree she caught one of the lower branches and swung herself out of the saddle, cheered by a band of Commandos who were climbing those dangerous cliffs for practice. The horse, so suddenly relieved of his burden, slowed and stopped in surprise, and the girl escaped with only badly wrenched shoulder muscles.

The Commandos were the great sensation of the village, but I could never bear to watch their dangerous exercises, one of which ended with a fatal casualty. We met these cheerful lusty young men everywhere, and their confidence in themselves inspired confidence in me. One morning we were disturbed early by a fierce grunting and squealing outside the caravan. I looked out to see a peculiarly filthy and repulsive sow with angry red eyes and yellow tusks rooting and tearing up the turf. She had wandered from the farm "up over" where I had seen her with a litter of baby pigs. Being country-bred I knew that a sow in pig, and after she has pigged, can be an ugly-tempered brute, and so seizing a long mountain-climbing stick, and shutting the enraged Blackness safely in the caravan, I ventured forth to drive this one away before she ruined our caravan site. It was a long business to induce her to descend the tor, but with some skill and much subtlety of manoeuvre I at last succeeded in herding her through the bracken to the gate in the valley. From there the lane wound uphill, past our seven-piece gate tied up with string, (which we opened as seldom as possible for these reasons), and so to her home-farm and her neglected family. Hot but triumphant I got her through the gate, closed it, and began the steep ascent back to the caravan. There, to my horror, I met — the sow!

Six laughing Commandos were standing in the lane.

"You'd lost your pig," said one. "We've got her back for you!"

They had cut all the lovely cords which secured our fragments of gate to form a whole, and had driven the sow through it and back to the caravan site . . . !

"She isn't much of a beauty," remarked another of them. "She could do with a wash."

"Whiffy is what she is," another unnecessarily informed me. "Concentrated Essence of Swine."

"Funny pets you keep, ma'am," commented a dark giant. "She don't somehow seem in keeping with that posh caravan."

When they had finished baiting me I explained to them the enormity of their offence. Not only *en croyant de bien faire*, had they returned to me an extremely offensive pig which it had taken me at least half an hour to remove, but they had destroyed all the careful work on our derelict bits of gate which had taken hours to bind securely into one piece, and which now lay in ruins at my feet.

They laughed uproariously, and I laughed ruefully.

"Well, ma'am," chuckled the largest of the six, "we meant well, and now we must make things ship-shape before we leave you. First — the pig."

The scared and enraged animal was immediately

surrounded, ambushed, chivvied and finally hunted, squealing with rage through the gate and up the lane. The din was indescribable, made up of barks of excitement from the imprisoned Dominie, and yells and shouts of laughter from the hunters where the sow charged one or other of them. Finally, as the pig grunted and waddled its way homeward, they all returned, and with coils of rope hidden in their tunics for climbing purposes, they lashed together our seven fragments of gate more securely than ever it had been before. While splicing and knotting they told us many interesting things — though of course nothing of their war exercises. They were filled with admiration for the exploits of a girl who had been sent down by the War Office to rob the falcons' eggs from their nests in the rock cliffs. Carrier pigeons with important messages had failed to reach their objective, and several rings had been found in the nest of a falcon. The falcon hawks had been destroying the pigeons as they neared the English shore. This girl would descend the cliffs from any dizzy height with only a cord around her. The men had seen her swung out over the edge of Gallantry Bower, Clovelly, and clinging to the face of the cliff with what foothold she could get, she then quietly searched for falcons' nests in the crevices of the rocks.

"She goes where some of my young recruits wouldn't dare go," said their leader. She's got guts, that girl, and no mistake. I take off my hat to her."

"Some of them girls down there are good plucked 'uns," remarked another man, jerking a thumb towards the Abbey, and then he recounted to me the episode of the bolting horse. "Monkeys, they call 'em. Well, I'd say that girl had monkey blood in her veins, swinging 'erself up into the tree like that."

"Funny place, Hartland, to plant a lot of high-spirited girls like them," observed another. "Dead end of nowhere."

I explained to them that the founder of the club considered that it was most important for young girls to be as sheltered and well fed as possible until they reached the age when they had to go and take their part in this hideous war.

"She's thinking of them as the mothers of the future," I said. "She's developing them mentally and physically for that. There's the future to consider."

There was a silence, and then the leader said:

"Wise woman that must be," and his companions stared into space. . . .

But for the presence of the Commandos in the neighbourhood and the manoeuvres of the Home Guard, a splendid band of hefty yeomen, young farmers and farm hands who knew every inch of their beloved County of Devon, and, later, the occasional appearance of hedge-hopping aeroplanes piloted by young Americans and taking hair-raising risks in our wooded valley, one could never have realised that one was living in a country at war. We were properly invaded and, as we were told afterwards, captured by a body of the Home Guard early one morning. The invasion exercise so interrupted the ordered routine of the Abbey that an irate London parlourmaid, striving to cope with breakfast for many Monkeys and constantly impeded by young men armed with sticks, staves and obsolete guns, who sprang upon each other from dark cupboards and corridors and seized this opportunity to settle private feuds, was at last goaded into speech. She remarked acidly:

"Couldn't we now be considered to be all *dead* and allowed to get on with our work?"

We were never safe from invasion of beasts, birds and small boys. There was the episode of the pig; and one day when I was intently occupied by some culinary preparations on my knees outside the caravan, I was startled nearly out of my wits by a sudden whir of wings as one of the famous white peacocks from the Abbey flew out from the hedge nearly into my face. Owls of all kinds sat on our gates and hooted in the trees by night; hawks of every variety wheeled and dived over and into the woods as of old; rabbits scuttled in the bracken. There was a little stone-built summer house with a fireplace and a bow-window on our site, and this I used at first as a dressing-room and writing-room, and finally slept in it during the winter. One day, while I was dressing, a small boy, evidently with an enquiring mind, suddenly entered without previously knocking on the door, swinging a naked skinned rabbit. He was lucky not to find me in the same condition when he delivered our Sunday luncheon.

We were invaded by occasional tourists whose progeny were mad to examine the caravan. Once by a wounded Wren who had been sent on sick leave to Hartland, had borrowed a horse from the farm where she was billeted, and had been dislodged with a bump. The children of the village wandered around the site with their parents hoping to be invited within the "Ark," and relays of Monkeys, often bringing their fathers, mothers, aunts and cousins, were our constant visitors when the founder of the club instituted a holiday course for parents, giving them wonderful concerts from musicians imported from London, lectures on literature, art and other subjects. I was invited to attend any of these that interested me, and I shall never forget my consternation on entering the Abbey to read the programme pinned up in the hall to see —

"*Item* 4. Something about Provence, by Lady Fortescue."

I stormed into the founder's study.

"What does this mean, 'Something about Provence,' by Lady Fortescue?" I asked her sternly. "I've never even been asked to talk to the girls, and I've no intention of doing so. Lecturing still terrifies me, and my life is hideous enough, giving these eternal talks for A.V.F."

She looked up from the pile of papers before her with a very sweet but mischievous smile.

"But, Peggy dear, all the members are so thrilled by the prospect of hearing you talk about France — you *couldn't* disappoint them now, you're much too kind-hearted, and you know you love my girls. *Of course* you'll talk to them on Wednesday night."

And of course I did.

In the same manner she blackmailed me into becoming a member of the Red Cross detachment she had formed for the girls and of which she was Commandant. In 1914 I was young and barely married, but wanting to fill my spare time with useful work I looked after "unwanted" babies in a crèche in Windsor, worked in a Y.M.C.A. canteen for soldiers, and, being quite untrained, did the dirty work in the hospital when drafts of wounded came in from the front, to set the skilled nurses free to do dressings and work. But I had never seemed to have time to attend Red Cross lectures or pass exams.

"I simply haven't time to mug up bandaging and home nursing now," I protested, when the Commandant approached me about this. "I have this terrifying programme of lectures to give, and I always come home afterwards feeling dead. I simply could NOT concentrate, and at my advanced age I refuse to risk being ploughed in elementary exams which your junior members will pass easily. I could never hold up my head again if such a shameful thing as that happened to me. Have *some* pity!"

"It is *because* you are *you* and because you *are* senior to them that they'll all want to join my detachment, and will work like demons if they are working with you," she riposted, "and every woman in England ought to be a member of the Red Cross at a time like this."

The first argument I doubted, but the second was unanswerable, and of course I joined the detachment.

Thenceforth every one who came near me had to be bandaged, and I drove to my lectures muttering the ridiculous names of bones and arteries, trying to remember poisons and their antidotes and the correct manner of laying out the dead. At any rate I now knew what would be done to me when these ghastly examinations finally killed me, which I felt must certainly be soon.

142

However, somehow I survived all the preliminary agony, and at last the dread day came when Doctor X was to come to the Abbey and examine us in an oral and practical manner. Happily he was already a friend of mine. When I first came to Hartland I was badgered by the rough edge of a tooth which was making my tongue very sore, and I knew that an open sore on the tongue could be dangerous. So I asked the nice wife of our grocer if Hartland possessed a resident doctor. "Oh yes," she replied. "There's Doctor X who lives just over the way — it's his surgery hour just now."

I crossed the road, entered the open door, and took my place at the end of a row of out-patients awaiting their turn to enter the doctor's consulting-room. Mine came at last, and I went in. The doctor, a dark man of middle height with dark vivacious eyes, looked me over critically, wondering no doubt who this new patient might be and what ailed her. I told him about the jagged back tooth.

"A dentist seems indicated," he remarked, with a twinkle.

"Yes, I know, but I haven't enough petrol to drive sixteen miles to the nearest town just to have a tooth filed. I wondered if *you'd* got an implement?" I said. "In any case, will you please give me an antiseptic mouth-wash for a sore tongue before I develop cancer?"

"Yes, I could do that, and even throw in a bit of emery paper for you to do your own filing," he replied. "But a dentist would probably do it better."

While he was packing up mouth-wash and the emery paper he remarked:

"I've never seen you before. Are you living in Hartland?"

"In a caravan in the woods of the Abbey."

"Do you always live in a caravan and choose damp places?" he enquired, with a quizzical look at my grey curls.

"You see, my real home is in France," I explained.

"France? What part of France?"

"In Provence."

Suddenly he was galvanised into activity. "Provence? Look here, I *must* lend you my favourite book. I keep it by my bed. It's all about Provence," he shouted excitedly as he shot upstairs. He returned breathlessly, and put into my hands a book entitled *Perfume from Provence*.

"It's an adorable book — a delicious book," he babbled. "When the war is over, my wife and I plan to take a holiday in Provence and visit all the lovely places this woman talks about."

Embarrassed though I was I couldn't repress a smile.

"Oh! You've *read* it!" he said disappointedly.

"Well — I wrote it," I confessed.

"YOU wrote it?" he almost shouted. "This is the most extraordinary coincidence. My favourite book, and the writer actually in my surgery. Well, I'll be damned. Look here," running to his desk, "you simply MUST autograph it for me." I did. In farewell I asked him the amount of his fee.

"FEE?" he said. "How could I accept a fee when I owe you for so many hours of delight?"

"No," I said firmly, *"Les affaires sont les affaires,* as

we say in France, and 'the labourer is worthy of his hire,' as you say in England. I came here unannounced as an ordinary out-patient. I might have been just Mrs. Jinks, and, as you say, it's pure coincidence that I chance to be the author of a book you like. Certainly I pay the usual fee for a consultation, and if you persist in refusing it I shall be obliged to die untended in my caravan if I get pneumonia in those damp woods, for I should certainly never send for *you*."

Reluctantly he stated the sum of one shilling and sixpence, and when I paid it said he should keep the money as a mascot.

Mrs. Jinks and the doctor had since become great friends, and therefore it was with relief that I heard that he would be our Red Cross examiner. He would certainly pull my leg, but there was a good hope that he might be lenient. On the day of the examination I was as nervous as I had always been on a first night — ridiculous at my age, I know. However, I got through my oral examination with flying colours, and the doctor smiled with pleasure as I answered his not very easy questions correctly. Then came the practical part. He asked me for a certain bandage, and deftly I bound up a volunteer Monkey who was supposed to be injured. Though I say it I did a neat bit of work. Then I stood back and looked at the doctor, expectant of approbation. I was proud of my bandage. Something in his look shook my confidence.

"That's the right way to bandage a broken scapula?" I asked him anxiously.

"Certainly it is," he replied, with a twinkle. Unsatisfied

I took his arm. "I must speak to you outside before you start on the next candidate," I hissed in his ear. Obediently he followed me out of the room.

"Look here," I said urgently, "you've GOT to tell me NOW if I've passed or failed. Because if I've failed I'm going straight back to the caravan to pack up and go away for ever, because I couldn't face the Commandant or a crowd of victorious little Monkeys. I can't wait for three days to know the results, and I didn't at all like the look in your eye when I'd finished that bandage. *What* was wrong with it? Tell poor Mrs. Jinks. I thought I'd done a really beautiful scapula bandage."

"You did," answered the doctor gently, "it was a perfect bandage. But you see I asked you to bind up a broken CLAVICLE."

I stared at him aghast. Then ga-ga-dom could start in the fifties. In fact, with me, it had.

"Sheer nerves," he comforted me. "That might happen to anyone. Your work was excellent even if mistaken, and in any case you didn't put a foot wrong in your oral. Of course you've passed, Mrs. Jinks."

"Ohhhhhhhhhh!" I sighed with gusty relief. "Then I can stay in Hartland."

And so it was that I became a member of the British Red Cross.

CHAPTER
SEVENTEEN

Plymouth Rock

I am not at all a "pi" person, but I know that God takes care of me and tries to teach me. Why He should take so much trouble over anyone so insignificant I can't imagine, but I try to show gratitude by not saying "Please" too often and never forgetting to say "Thank you." I have learned to keep my eyes and ears open for His signs and messages, for He has very often gently slapped this tiresome child of His with symbols. For example, once when I had to suffer almost unendurable and continued physical pain while alone in Paris having treatment for my mysterious poison, I was guilty of a very cowardly thought; I had even one leg slipping over the edge of that terrible abyss of self-pity. I lay with eyes closed wishing that I could die, and so be done for ever with physical pain and the mental agony of having become an expense to my beloved man, whom I had tried so hard to help. Suddenly I opened my eyes and there, on the wall beside my bed, was a gigantic black cross standing stark against a background of dazzling golden light. Then it disappeared. That vision startled me into shame. What was my little spot of suffering compared with His . . . ?

The material explanation of my vision was — very material. My bedroom faced the Eiffel Tower, which had been hired by the Citröen Car Company for electrical advertisement, and at night CITRÖEN and the date of its foundation flashed intermittently in thousands of electric lamps. This dazzling light shone upon my wall through the uncurtained window whose reflected architraves formed a huge black cross. All the same, *I* knew that I had been slapped by a symbol, and I hastily drew up that slipping leg.

That is only one example of many reminders and stimulants that all my life I have received. There have been times when, like every human being, I have badly needed stimulation, and always encouragement has come from some completely unexpected source at the blackest of black periods. For instance when, to my amazement, I learned that my first book, *Perfume from Provence*, had met with instant success. To have written a best-seller when it could no longer help my man was like the bitterness of death. I could feel no interest in my sudden fame, and thought drearily that I would never write another word since what I earned could no longer be of use to him. Then, when I had to come to London on business, I dined one night with a very dear friend. I told him all this. His face suddenly lit up, and he said: "But think how *terribly* proud of you Sir John is now!" That was a golden straw which saved a drowning woman. Then, some weeks later when, back in France, I was having my *petit déjeuner* in bed, my letters were brought to me. I opened a thin foreign envelope addressed in an unknown hand, and a thin trickle of golden sand peppered my breakfast tray. I pulled forth a page evidently torn from a notebook, and read a pencilled message. It was headed:

"From an Englishwoman camping in the Sahara," and she said:

"In the last paragraph of your book you say that *Monsieur* never knew that he was leaving you alone. This is to tell you that you are *not* alone. All your readers are with you — and you're teaching us how to live."

Teaching my readers how to live? *I* teaching anybody anything? Quite amazing, and would have been ignored by me as a pleasant nothing had I heard such a thing by word of mouth. But there was the foreign envelope, the torn page — and, above all, the golden desert sand. It was a *real* message from a real woman camping in the wonderful silence of the desert.

Well — if in some mysterious way I could still help people with my pen — then life was still worth living, and I would go on writing. . . .

Dear unknown Englishwoman, that message scribbled in your tent or under the stars sitting by your camp fire, brought back to me the incentive to write which *Monsieur* took away with him. You sent me a star to guide me in my desert.

And now the same wonderful thing happens again. Once more I seemed to have come to a dead end. I was feeling that awful sense of the futility of all human effort, a terrible numbness of spirit, no ideas in my head, no desire to work, inspiration dead — when another letter, written by a person unknown, brought me back to life. It was a message addressed to me care of my publishers, and was from the matron and sister tutor of an enormous much-blitzed hospital in Plymouth. They told me that they had worried terribly over my fate, and had always rushed to greet the ambulances bringing in injured passengers from torpedoed or bombed ships, fearing that I might be one of the victims. They had ceaselessly questioned all refugees from France, but could get no news of me. Through my books they had learned to love me. All this touched me deeply, but the concluding sentence I shall keep always in my heart:

"We think you might like to know that when we had those awful Blitzes here, every evening before they began we always read a chapter of one or other of your books. When we were too busy to read we quoted to each other our favourite passages. And so we gained some measure of serenity, courage to face the horror of the night to come, and hope for the future."

To have brought some comfort to such gallant women at such a time filled me with a very humble thankfulness — and once again I was spurred on to write. First I wrote to thank them for what they had done for me, and told them that, lying in my caravan on the heights of Dartmoor, I had watched the terrible glow of fire turning the sky above their seaport a lurid red and heard the awful explosions of bombs, and I had prayed for all who must live and work in that hell. Curious that we were all thinking of one another at that time.

Hearing that I was in Devon, they wrote again begging me to go and see them if I were ever anywhere near, and later, when speaking at a public meeting in their town, I telephoned to them that I was near, and they pressed me to come and address the hospital staff, who all longed to hear about France from me.

So I went — but when I entered the gates of that vast building I very nearly turned tail and fled. In fact I was hesitating on the lowest of a most imposing flight of steps when a little thin, flying figure wearing nurse's uniform, who proved to be the sister tutor, came leaping down the steps like a chamois, and, seizing both my hands, drew me impulsively upwards and into the hospital. I was taken straight to the matron, who, although a reserved Scot, honoured me by welcoming me like an old friend.

Those nurses were a lovely audience and became staunch allies, helping me to collect money for the Fighting French. Afterwards, as I descended that long flight of steps into the courtyard, where my chairman was waiting to drive me off to another engagement, I wistfully wished that I could have a nice gentle little accident at that moment and be carried back into the atmosphere of warmth and love I had just left.

In a letter I told matron of that secret wish, and she wrote at once to beg me, if I could ever escape or find a lull in my storm of engagements, to go and stay in her little flat in the hospital as her guest. "We are very worried about you. You are so thin and you look so deadly tired. Do come and let us spoil you a little. You could stay in bed all the time — remember that carrying trays is half of our job. . . ."

There came a moment when I did accept this invitation, and the happy week I spent in that hospital is the brightest of my war memories. The assistant matron was away, and I occupied her flat. In the bedroom and sitting-room I found flowers everywhere. In the bathroom a cake of FRENCH soap, a bottle of FRENCH perfume, a jar of FRENCH bath salts and a tin of FRENCH talcum powder; treasures hoarded from short pre-war holidays in France and now lavished upon me. By my bed were peppermint bulls' eyes, my favourite biscuits, my favourite drink, Craven A cigarettes, even lilies of the valley — my favourite flower. Indeed these dear people *had* studied the babblings in my books. Every morning sister tutor brought me my breakfast tray, and every day I found upon it a tiny "Perfume from Provence" posy of flowers, beautifully arranged by her. Never have I been so spoiled, never have I found it harder to say good-bye.

During that week, always in joking conversation and from anecdotes laughingly exchanged, I learned much of the heroism of that hospital staff during those awful Blitzes (mercifully there were none during my visit, though once or twice the sirens wailed). In the midst of a raid, when bombs were raining on the hospital, and part of the roof and a reservoir of water had been destroyed, matron, marching with her Scottish dignity through chaos, met a nurse without a cap.

"Where is your cap, sister?" she demanded severely, for even with hell let loose discipline must be maintained.

"Matron, where is yours?" gently replied the sister, with a twinkle in her eyes. Both caps had been blown away by blast.

Matron, wandering on through the wreckage, met a

little nurse who lodged in an annexe and was off duty that night.

"Why aren't you in your shelter, nurse?" she enquired.

"Matron, there isn't any shelter now," the child replied.

Intent upon her duty as matron of this huge hospital, the undaunted woman made a tour of every ward. All the electric plant had been blown to blazes, and she made her brave pilgrimage nearly always in darkness. Constantly she was seized by unseen hands and forced to the floor as bombs burst quite near, for she refused to take cover.

"Can you imagine the matron of a hospital on all fours? How could I take cover?" she asked me laughingly. "But, oh, my arms were bruised next day by the assaults of my staff."

One of these was fatally injured, lying with eyes closed on the floor of a ward. As matron bent over her she heard this gasping prayer:

"O God, take care of matron, she's got so much to do to-night."

That nearly broke her down.

Going in search of her "babies" — little probationers and V.A.D.s — she found them all in a dim corridor quietly laying out the civilian dead who had been brought in from the town and had since died of injuries. No one had thought of occupying inexperienced children with such a task, but in their little Red Cross manual they had learned how to perform those last offices for the dead — and someone had to do this work, so they banded together and did it.

Under a blazing staircase sat a pale child beside a wounded man. Ordered by matron to save herself quickly, she replied that the man had an injured back and she had been told to stay by him and not on any account to move him or let him be moved until a doctor came with stretcher-bearers. Then had come a rain of incendiary bombs — but that looked a pretty solid staircase and help would certainly be here soon.

Fantastic things happened that night. A convent of the town had been bombed, and wounded and shell-shocked nuns had been brought into the hospital for treatment. Every women's ward, the floor of every ward, and every corridor was filled with casualties. The only floor space left was in the men's ward, and here matron found a striped effect of men and nuns all lying in line — a man, then a nun, another man and then another nun, the whole length of the ward.

True Scot to the backbone, every drop of her blood infused with the courage, modesty and justice of her race, matron steadily refused the decoration for gallantry offered to her later, saying with truth that each of her nurses deserved it equally — and after all, they had only done their duty.

In Plymouth I found everywhere that invincible spirit. Around the crater of what had once been the residence of the Admiral of the Port, bombed to blazes — fortunately while he and his wife were elsewhere — he had planted a particular species of bean, renowned for the nourishment it gives. He gave me a handful of these to plant for France, with strict instructions not to be tempted to eat them myself when tender and green, but to keep them for seed. He gave them to everybody, and told me ruefully that one aged peer to whom he had presented the precious seed forgot all about his injunctions to keep his harvest for starving Europe, and appeared one day with a full basket of young and tender *primeurs*, which he presented proudly to the Admiral as a delicacy for his dinner.

Walking through the streets of Plymouth I came upon the roofless skeleton of a great church banked around by masses of sandbags. Anxious to see how far its interior was damaged, I asked a policeman if I might climb up the barricade and look through one of the gaping arches which once had been windows. With a little secret smile and a nod of assent he gave his permission, and I clambered up.

Inside I saw not a scene of utter desolation but a lovely garden. Green turf replaced the paving of the aisles, flowers of every hue were planted below the great grey pillars, up which climbed rambler roses. The chancel also had become a garden and the undamaged altar had been removed into a corner of a side aisle where still a fragment of roofing could shelter it. In such a place it would be very easy to worship God under His lovely blue sky and amid His flowers. I felt a longing to meet the rector of that church who had made a garden from a crater, and, defying the Devil and all his works; still ministered to his flock in that lovely place.

"And He shall give them Beauty for Ashes."

CHAPTER
EIGHTEEN

The Circle of Peace

Often during those months in Devon, in the quiet of the woods or when driving to some public engagement, and always when one of our aeroplanes roared through the sky, I thought of Richard Hillary and wondered what had become of him. His silence saddened me, but I felt that whatever happened to either of us we should always be friends, for we had understood each other instantly and perfectly. I had become suddenly so busy, rushing from place to place, that I had no time to write letters. Richard was probably busier still. It was at any rate comforting to have seen him last in much better condition, with no dread repetition of a surgical operation hanging immediately over him. Those last joyous words to me, "I've got a job! I've GOT A JOB!" comforted me then so much. It was a very long time afterwards that I learned from his mother, who had then become a dear friend, that he had spoken so often of me and in such terms that my name had become very sacred in their home; but he had been rushed off to the United States to do propaganda work to speak on platforms all over America; of the stand England was making all alone; of the work of the R.A.F.; the Battle of Britain. He had been so keen to go, to try to make them see their own danger and join us as allies. But that job and that visit caused him only bitterness of spirit; for when the British Minister in Washington saw the terrible disfigurement of that beautiful boy, he decided that he must never speak from platforms lest his appearance shock American mothers and make them resolve never to allow *their* sons to become airmen. Richard might speak — but only into a microphone. How that verdict must have hurt those nerves of his! Richard, who refused all semblance of pity with such gallant defiance, and who insisted upon being accepted as an ordinary individual — to be treated as a freak or an unpleasant deformity and allowed to speak to America only through a microphone! During one of our talks he had told me that very soon after his smash, "When I was a much worse mess than I am now and they hadn't started 'arranging' me," he had invited all his pre-war friends who hadn't seen him since his accident to a cocktail party in London. "I was curious to see their reaction. After ten minutes I paid the bill and walked out on them. I didn't want the 'Oh! you POOR darling!' coupled with looks of horror that were showered upon me."

As I listened I knew that he had wanted to test their friendship; to see if they could still recognise the shining spirit of him behind the marred face; to find out which of them, if any, realised that looks matter not at all and that the REAL RICHARD was unchanged. Still — it was rather a brutal test, for we are all human, and, although *I* had instantly sensed what he was, it had been an effort to disguise all feeling of horror and pity for what he must have suffered to be so terribly disfigured. Later he became softer and more lenient. I remember saying to him one evening in farewell, "You'll find that you gained more than you lost through this accident," and his instant answer, "Yes. I'm finding that out already."

I told him of my correspondence with Luke Paget, that beloved and most understanding of men, then Bishop of Chester, at the darkest moment of my life. I had lost Mummie, and my old war-poison was causing hideous expense to my man, whom I had tried so hard to help until drastic treatments rendered this impossible. I told the Bishop that I had become spiritually dead; that when partaking of the Sacrament, that tender, beautiful service which had once meant so much to me, I found myself wondering what our cook would give us for breakfast. I told him that I wanted to murder people who looked at me with pity in their eyes. I had a savage desire to shock him by telling the bald truth. But he wasn't shocked at all. He realised that I needed help and comfort so terribly; he saw that wavering hand of mine stretching towards him out of the sea of bitter sorrow that was engulfing me. And he seized it and helped me to fight my way back to the rock of Faith. He begged me to permit people to be kind to me, urged me to try to relax and let things take their course, telling me that scientists and psychologists had proved that to fight against illness and to reject sympathy only aggravated the ills and shut one away from the healing power of love.

Richard had listened, moving about in rebellious restlessness at first, but finally he had given me a little nod and a grin. Then, to change a subject which had perhaps become unbearably intimate, he repeated a remark he was continually making; looking at his marred hands, and then keenly at me, he asked:

"Oh, *do* you think I shall ever handle a stick again?"

At the back of his mind, and always in his heart, was a longing to fly again: to join once more the comradeship of the Knights of the Air, singing as he flew: ". . . that moment have we passed into a sort of oneness, and our state is like a floating spirit's."

"Write that book first, Richard," I repeated urgently. "During your convalescence write that book — and by the time it is written you *may* be able to fly again."

Down in Devon I often wondered about the fate of that book. Had he written it? And then one day some friends came to tea with me in my caravan, and while talking about "shoes and ships and sealing-wax and cabbages and kings," one of them suddenly asked me if I had read that wonderful new book *The Last Enemy* — the Book Society's choice for the month, the first edition of twenty-five thousand copies sold out immediately — an extraordinary book written by a young airman who had crashed badly.

A hand — a maimed hand — seemed to squeeze my heart as I listened in silence.

"What is the name of the author?" I asked — quite unnecessarily.

"Richard Hillary," was the answer.

Suddenly it seemed to me that all creatures that on earth do dwell were singing to the Lord with an even more joyful voice than usual. The bird-song in the woods swelled into a chorus of praise and thanksgiving, the grasshoppers chirped more cheerfully, and when I bent down to whisper to The Blackness, "Dominie, he's DONE it! OUR boy has written his book and the world has acclaimed it," he laughed up in my face, and, seizing the large slice of cake I lavished upon him to celebrate this great occasion, leaped from the caravan out into the sunshine, tore madly round amid the bracken in ever-narrowing circles, then sank down in the centre to devour his delicacy in peace.

The centre of the circles of peace — Richard's phrase. In writing his book, expressing his personality and pent-up emotion, had Richard found that peace of the soul that passeth understanding and surely would be found in the centre of those circles? And then I remembered his oft-repeated question, "Shall I ever handle a stick again?" and my answer, "Write that book first, Richard . . . and by the time it is written you may be able to fly again."

The book was written and was a triumphant success. One ambition achieved. There still remained the last and greatest. Deep within me I knew that although Richard had achieved sudden fame as a writer, and had now the literary world at his feet, an honourable profession ahead of him which despite his physical disabilities he could pursue in the peace of his own home close to those parents who understood and adored him, his soaring spirit could not be content with that while England, the world and his own particular comrades of the air were still in danger. Nevertheless, he had already done more than his duty. He had suffered — and had been terribly maimed in the cause of England — surely those poor hands of his would never be permitted to handle a stick again? He was so young. A mere baby. . . . So the woman in me argued and pleaded while the voices of my fighting ancestors strove to convince me that Richard Hillary, despite his youth, was made of sterner stuff. A mere literary success could never content him. He was "The Happy Warrior" personified.

I awaited his letter telling me of his achievement — or perhaps he would just send me a copy of THE book which we had so often discussed. I waited in vain, but though human enough to be disappointed, nevertheless I knew that in spite of the disparity of age, nothing could change the friendship between us, and that when we met again we should just pick up the threads that had been so suddenly dropped, and, with laughter, knot them together.

But that will not be yet. The web of Richard's destiny, woven with silver moonlight, spangled with stars, glittering and glorious is already woven into a perfect circle — long ago he reached the centre of the circles of peace. . . . "I saw eternity the other night like a great ring of pure and endless light. . . ."

The news of his passing came to me when I was in a sunlit clearing of the woods of Hartland watching the hawks wheeling and swooping suddenly from the sky. So had he wheeled and swooped unerringly upon his prey.

With a deep pride I learned that he had carelessly thrown aside the literary fame so swiftly gained. Deaf to the pleas of his publisher urging him to complete his second book, scarcely begun, for which the public clamoured; defying some of his doctors; over-persuading others with his steely will, he had gained the wish of his heart and joined once more the Gallant Company of the Air. And now that bright head of his is crowned by immortal bays, for joyously he sought and vanquished the last enemy, Death.

CHAPTER
NINETEEN

Personalities
and Dampness

The Rector of Hartland possesses a personality almost as tremendous as his great booming voice, which when let loose in St. Nectan's Church reverberated as powerfully as the organ, and I sometimes feared might threaten even the foundations of that famous beacon tower. His parish straggles over more undulating miles than most in England, with but few important houses within it, so that the problem of church expenses is always acute. But he is an indomitable man with an original mind and tremendous energy, and he contrives to make money in a variety of ways. For example, he organised a summer fête — a daring thing to do in the extremely moist West Country. To lure the great personages of Devon from their ancestral homes to remote Hartland he must produce an attraction of considerable magnitude, and for some time he hesitated between the popular curves of Mae West and the Oriental splendour of the Emperor of Abyssinia, who, finally chosen, consented to come if his expenses were paid with a fee of five guineas for the benefit of his poor country. I should most certainly have considered this to be "a tall story" had I not been shown photographs of the Emperor — clad, alas! in European dress — shivering in the rain beside the lord and lady of the manor. Of course it rained on the great day.

Another method of raising funds was by the sale of sugar sweets boxed in tins labelled with a picture of St. Nectan's. The Rector gained the necessary permit, and made an arrangement with the manufacturers to sell him sweets at the wholesale rate, which, when the necessary coupons were produced, he re-sold at the usual retail price, giving the balance to his church. In the embrasures of the church he stood beautiful little cardboard models of St. Nectan's with a slit in the roof of the tower into which pennies, silver or notes could be poked; the most attractive form of collecting box I ever saw. He was filled with new ideas which involved hours spent in correspondence and vast sums in postage, but the result of his original schemes and appeals always justified the outlay. This energy and devotion would have been remarkable in a young man, but demonstrated untiringly by a man who had certainly reached and maybe passed the age of three score and ten years was, to me, staggering.

He paid a formal visit to the caravan one day, and his first remark was uttered in a tone of dry sarcasm, redeemed by a twinkle in very keen eyes.

"You have a fine view of the OUTSIDE of St. Nectan's," he said.

Never once since my return to Hartland had I been able to attend the only service (which was held in the morning) because of the tiresome treatment I always have to do, and petrol being so precious and limited, I had never been able to drive to the evening service in the church in Hartland Village. My prayers and praises to the Creator of all Beauty were said and sung with the birds and beasts in the woods of Hartland, The Blackness generally yowling louder than anyone.

Whether The Blackness lived a blameless life when absent from my side I shall never know, but one day I had grave doubts about the chastity of which I had always boasted. He had been extraordinarily restless for days, hanging his head out of the caravan windows and sniffing frantically when shut in at night, seeking any excuse or none to slink off into the bracken and make good his escape — where? — by day. Generally he returned in time for his dinner, but on this occasion we saw no sign of him all day long. We had heard of traps set for rabbits in hedges — we had been warned that the Commandos sometimes collected cats and dogs, found at large, and kept them as mascots; those dangerous cliffs — search parties were organised, the Monkeys from the Abbey gave zealous help, and I tramped the tors and lanes calling, calling and following false clues given by good-natured farmers who had seen "a lil' black dawg" some time since. In the end, still far from home, without a torch and fearing to get lost in lonely places in the gathering mist, I plodded wearily back to the caravan, giving a mournful imitation of my home-made yodel which never, so far, had failed to call him back to my side. No reply. No little Blackness. Sadly I pushed open the door of the caravan — and there he was, lying on one of the bunks, beat to the world, an exhausted, bedraggled Blackness, soaking wet *all over*. That was the sinister thing. The weather was then fine and dry, and we well knew that when bathing he NEVER immersed his head or back. My companion was on her knees rubbing him dry. When hope had faded she had suddenly seen a completely exhausted Dominie striving to climb the tor, and had rushed out to carry him home.

From that moment I had a strong suspicion that there *might* now be a blot on the family escutcheon, but, since a very pathetic episode in Sussex, I had learned that such suspicions concerning The Blackness could be cruelly unjust. A friend had taken him for a very long walk right through the woods and far beyond the danger zone of red setters. He had a marvellous time, but when she turned to go home he had vanished. She searched, she called, she retraced her steps, but Dominie was nowhere to be seen. Despairingly she realised that he had indeed given her the slip, and, as it was growing dusk, she was obliged to come back to "Many Waters" — and me — without him. We were less nervous about his unprotected return, for after dark the red setters would be indoors, and very late in the evening he came back. There were many lovely canine ladies secluded at that moment, and I had been warned that in the spring my Blackness would certainly burst bounds and go and serenade them, so perhaps he had been playing troubadour. Some days later, when he had again successfully dodged my friend and done his disappearing trick, she determined next time never to take her eyes off him during the walk, and to stalk him from a discreet distance to find out where he *did go*. Dominie led her a dance that afternoon, through woods and undergrowth, over ploughed fields and through thick-set hedges. Often she lost him for a time while searching for an aperture, stile or gate when he had squirmed through hawthorn and brambles. But always she pursued, and was rewarded by the sight of a small determined Blackness trotting ever onward towards his mysterious objective. At last he turned down a narrow cart track leading to a farmhouse. Here he paused, flickered his tail expectantly and gave a short sharp bark outside the garden gate, which was soon afterwards opened by the farmer's wife, who greeted him as an old friend. My companion waited a few moments, realising that he had reached his journey's end, and then stealthily crept up to the gate and peeped over it. There was my Blackness romping madly with a diminutive puppy and a tiny kitten, which, at intervals in the game, he picked up with his velvet spaniel's mouth and carried across the little lawn. He had grown tired of being an only child, and had found his own playfellows. The farmer's wife said that his visits were frequent. Always he announced his arrival with the same little bark, was admitted, romped with his friends until he was tired, and then she opened the gate and said, "Now, Dominie, you must go home," and off he plodded in the direction of "Many Waters." She had read my name and address on his tail-waggers' badge, but having no telephone could not reassure me about his whereabouts. Troubadour indeed! What could have been more divinely innocent?

And so, even after that Hartland episode, I continued to give him the benefit of the doubt. But all the same, my lonely Blackness must soon be provided with a little wife. It is not good that man should live alone, nor would the weather always remain fine and dry for the search parties. It was not long, in fact, before there came a change.

Is there anywhere else in the world where it rains as it can rain in Devon? When the leaden skies poured down upon us, the ground around the caravan became water-logged, the three-gallon cans we stood under its tiny rain-pipes filled and over-brimmed in a night, and to reach the Abbey we had to wade through lakes of water in the park. I was sure that beloved Hartland must be the wettest place in the universe. I was equally sure that our Devon rain, soft, caressing rain, was nicer rain than anyone else's rain as I sloshed through the sodden woods to the garage near the Abbey farm where my little Grey Pigeon was tucked up snugly in bad weather. But I did not enjoy those wet and windy drives across country to reach the school, college, rotary club or women's institute where an audience awaited me; nor the return drive, often in the dark, rather exhausted by speaking, meeting new people and taking note of their addresses, and the questions I must answer. The caravan was as well built as a caravan could be, but when the bad weather really set in we decided that a tarpaulin covering the roof would prevent rain driving in through the ventilators, and I had the brilliant idea of utilising the huge green waterproofed canvas awning supplied as an extra and supposed to be attached as a protection from the sun if one wanted to sit or eat out of doors. As trees provided shade on our present site, this awning had never been used, and together my companion and I spent a whole afternoon stretching the unwieldy covering over the domed roof of the caravan, and securing it on all sides with ropes and stout pegs.

We were delighted with our work until one of Hartland's famous Atlantic gales roared and shrieked down upon us one stormy night. Sheltered though we were by woods and a tor behind us, the caravan was rocked like a boat, and our improvised tarpaulin slapped and banged overhead, and, when the wind got under it, threatened to act as a sail and swirl us up into the Infinite. The noise was deafening and perfectly maddening because intermittent. There would be a long lull, and just as we were drowsing off to sleep, another wild gust of wind would start the slapping and banging of that cursed tarpaulin again.

"*Not* a success, our tarpaulin," shouted my companion through the partition, but made no suggestion how the nuisance might be abated — because, in such a gale, there *was* nothing to do about it, save to cut it adrift.

Brilliant idea! Cut it adrift! *I* would cut it adrift and that right speedily, for I could bear no more of this frightful din. Springing from my bunk I burst into the kitchen, and seizing a huge meat hatchet from a locker leaped out into the night and hacked those tethering ropes. The tarpaulin slid heavily to the ground, and after that there was peace. My friend has since told me that never before had she seen so weird and fantastic a spectacle as the lady of the caravan, the wind whipping her white nightdress and her silver curls into the air, tearing round the caravan in the gale brandishing a wicked-looking hatchet that glinted in the fitful light of the moon.

After the gale a glorious day, and then — more rain. The Monkey Club complained that in spite of it their water supply at the Abbey had mysteriously ceased. Investigation discovered that eels had floated up the flooded river and stopped up the supply pipe. This was an unusual but understandable reason for a water shortage, but what has always amazed, does amaze and will always amaze me is the perpetual water shortage in Devon in *spite* of so much rain. Rivers run low, springs run dry, cisterns are empty when you imagine that they will be brimming. Devonians when asked for an explanation of this mystery wag their heads sagely, and tell you that you must wait for the springs to break? When, how and why they break remains a mystery to me.

We weathered a very damp autumn, and then the founder of the Monkey Club and her partner insisted that I should live in the Abbey during December. I had not been well, and my companion urged me to accept the generous offer. Being younger and more robust, she herself decided to go on living in the caravan. By an odd coincidence I was given the room at the end of the corridor on the ground floor which, when we stayed in the Abbey, had always been allotted to John as his study. Here many chapters of his great *History of the British Army* had been written. Now it was converted into a lovely bed-sitting-room for me. I was spoiled in every way. My room was constantly invaded by eager girls, and while I was there I dressed *The Cradle Song*, which the members of the club acted for the benefit of the villagers — and the Red Cross — playing the part of Balthazar myself. All my chiffon winged tea-gowns were used to clothe angels, and we made glorious feathery wings for them with graduated sprays of silvery pampas grass. It was hard work creating something from nothing, but very great fun, and had the usual *succès fou* of all dramatic performances coached by the founder.

In the spring I returned to the caravan until one day business called me to London. I packed my soldier's *musette*, slung it over my shoulder, and promising The Blackness that I would be back in three days' time, drove away to Bideford.

In London I felt very, very odd. My back hurt, my tumpkin hurt, I had queer cramps in my arms and legs. Cramp in my *hands* — which must write — scared me, and I decided surreptitiously to visit a specialist while I was so conveniently near, and I did. He gave me a very thorough examination and then said: "You're on the verge of septicemia, and to avoid it must start treatment to-day." I looked at him aghast. "I hope you've been leading a very easy life," he went on; "any effort in your condition is dangerous." I smiled grimly. . . .

The old 1915 war poison rampant again. D—N!

"I'm only in London for three days, and then I must go back to Devon to fulfil dozens of important engagements," I protested.

"You will have important engagements with me, my nurses and my osteopath for six solid weeks, and then we'll cure you," he answered.

"At any rate, you'll have lots of fun," I retorted, I

suppose rather rudely, but he was the fifty-fourth doctor to promise a cure which never cured.

Well — I had to send a fleet of telegrams and then find lodgings, and the dreary treatments started. My companion of the caravan wrote depressed letters, and nearly broke my heart by telling me that my Blackness was refusing food and exercise, and sat in the window of the caravan overlooking the lane up which I should drive when I returned. I had promised him I would be back in three days, and he understood perfectly. When I did not come he imagined that some dire tragedy had befallen me, and was inconsolable. What could I do? How make him know that I was still alive and thinking of him?

Suddenly I knew. I would send him the vest that I wore. I stripped, tore off my vest and sent it off in a parcel addressed to him. It was a tremendous success. The moment the postman approached the caravan with his parcel Dominie rushed at him, sniffed it and seized it in his mouth. Then he lay down, and putting floppy paws upon it tore it open, afterwards racing madly round and round the caravan carrying my vest in his teeth. At night he took it to bed with him.

I gave orders that it should not be taken away or washed until I sent another at the end of the next week. Thenceforward he ate, went for joyous walks, and resigned himself to my prolonged absence. His mother was still alive and thinking of him. My little precious Blackness, I had never broken a promise to him before.

But I found life in London very dreary and lonely,

unable to work and deprived of my two companions, and then one day, when reading my favourite fragment of *The Times* — the Personal column, which always suggests such romantic possibilities to my imaginative mind — I happened to see that a little house within a few doors of my present lodgings was for sale or to be let furnished. Why not see if it could be hired for a short period and transport my family from Devon to share those last weeks of treatment with me? I called at the house, and discovered its owner to be the granddaughter of James Sant, the painter, who in his old age had painted a portrait of me, and whose familiar pictures adorned its walls. She would naturally have preferred to let it on a long lease, or to sell the house and have done with the responsibility of it, for she was now living in the country with her mother. But the strange coincidence of my knowing her father and other members of the family decided her, I think, to allow me to occupy it for a few weeks. I loved that little Adam house, and we were all very happy in it. A wonderful parlourmaid who had looked after John and me in London wrote to me at that moment. The war had transformed her into a clever cook-general, and, providentially, she asked if I knew of work with "someone like yourself?" Hastily I wrote to secure her, and Emily Darling came.

The problem of exercising The Blackness now exercised me. He would hate being towed along the streets of London, however alluring the lamp-posts, after running wild in Hartland. And then inspiration came. The little house was near the lovely grounds of Holland House. Since the historic house had been burned down, the garden had become a wilderness, but Dominie at least would prefer it in the wild state. I would ask the beloved Birdie Ilchester for permission to let him roam there with me. Permission was gladly given, and having secured safe and healthy exercise for my Blackness, I fixed the day for his journey.

Of course I went to meet the travellers, and when, at the end of a seemingly interminable train, I saw a little black blot amid passengers, porters and baggage, I resisted a wild desire to give his especial yodel and see what would happen. Only when I was within about twenty yards of him did I let it forth — with startling results. He went quite mad, reared, plunged and circled around cursing porters, winding his lead round their angry legs until he tore it from the hand of his guardian. Then he saw me and galloped with flying banner ears and floppy feet. I bent down to receive the longed-for welcome, and he literally fell upon and overbalanced me. Regardless of everybody and all the conventions, I remained sitting on the platform while we embraced. A lovely happy moment.

He approved our little house and took instant possession. The only thing that continued to scare him was the service lift, which suddenly and noiselessly rose from the floor of the dining-room, cleverly concealed by parquet. The owner of the house had warned me never to put a chair in that place and sit on it, or I might be propelled ceilingwards. The Blackness found it weird, and even though it brought him his dinner, as well as ours, he never became reconciled to it. Emily, discovering his intelligence and velvet mouth, used him as a messenger between kitchen, dining-room and bedrooms, putting little written messages into his mouth to save her legs. He brought them to me, and I sent back replies in the same way. My sister came to stay with us and, watching him, remarked: "Not only have you a noiseless service lift but also a dumb waiter."

He adored his walks in the vast wilderness around Holland House, splashing into the pools under the fountains, hunting for rabbits in the undergrowth. To me that dear place was haunted by ghosts. The last time I had seen it in full glory was when a ball was given for Mary, the eldest girl. Every window of the old house blazed with lights, and John and I had wandered in the rose-garden watching lovely girls in shimmering silks and cloudy chiffons walking down the stone steps, laughing happily with boys, many of whom must long since have been killed. Moonlight, roses, the muted music of violins made the scene like a romantic dream. In the great ballroom was everybody of any importance in London; the older women wearing glorious jewels and tiaras, the men full decorations, for two royal princes were present.

And now! Holland House a blackened ruin. The gardener told me that during the Battle of Britain he and his wife had moved from their lodge into the great house in case of incendiary bombs. On the night of the fire he had gone out on to the lawn to look around. The whole of the sky above London was a terrifying lurid red, and Holland House was outlined against it, every window reflecting the glare. He had just remarked to his wife that only a miracle could save such a target — when it was hit. All those historic treasures, all that loveliness gone in a night. The priceless panelling burned like tinder, and all that now remains are the outside walls, condemned as unsafe. Oh, what a tragedy. . . .

As Dominie and I walked over rough tussocky grass, once soft green shaven lawns, I had visions of Birdie, their children and many dogs joyously romping there; crowds of happy friends having tea on the terrace, John naming Benjy, Birdie's cocker spaniel, "The Profligate," because he often absented himself at night. Birdie, watching his long fingers tickling her little dog under his collar and noting the gentle and whimsical expression of his eyes as he upbraided the small black Don Juan, laughingly warning him that one day he and I might catch "Cockeritis," as, sure enough, we did. I suffer from it still. ("And so do *we*!" many of my readers will doubtless growl.)

CHAPTER
TWENTY

Joyous Release

Helped by *le bon Dieu*, The Blackness, my caravan companion and Emily Darling, at last I emerged from that particular tunnel. At intervals all our lives we have to go through dark tunnels, but if we try to ignore the enveloping darkness and steadily stare ahead there is always that arc of light to hearten us, and at last we find ourselves out in the sunlight again.

The worst of the winter was overpast and we could return to Devon. I had still several engagements to fulfil in the south — Torquay, Paignton and Brixham, that lovely little fishing-port which was now almost entirely peopled by French and Belgian fishermen and their families. One Breton family of seventy-two persons had arrived one night in their own boat, grandparents, uncles, aunts, cousins and children. Two of the women were about to present the world with little Fighting Frenchmen, and so the family midwife also had been brought along to see that all the necessary rites were performed in the French manner. That was so entirely French in its thoroughness that it amused me vastly. Our association of A.V.F. had to house them, clothe them, provide them with work, crèches for their babies, and schools to educate their children. We even supplied a little bar with a *zinc* and a motherly Frenchwoman to look after it, and the crowd of refugees who went there every evening felt more at home with one of their own countrywomen to joke with them and attend to their needs.

Homesick for France myself, the visit to Brixham was one of pure joy. To hear sabots clattering about the quays and snatches of French songs carolled light-heartedly from the fishing boats in the tiny harbour; to see the boxes of fish stacked beautifully neatly and not one fish head littering the paving stones, and inside the houses we had hired for the French the same exquisite order and cleanliness, little statues of saints on the mantelpiece, coquettish little curtains made from scraps, and an all-pervading smell of onion soup! It all warmed my heart, which had been terribly sad and apprehensive since the Germans had occupied the South of France and I was once again cut off from all my friends — and *Mademoiselle*.

When she last wrote to me she was ill. "I have septic carbuncles in all vital places, but I'm trying to keep the flag flying." Her letter had taken three weeks to write, for she had carbuncles inside her ears and each finger was bound up. Knowing how delicate she had been, I was in an agony about her now.

"We are all growing much too slim. Very difficult to console Squibs. Can you anyhow send parcels?" she had cabled later. And though I tried in every way, even writing and sending money to friends in Portugal, every avenue was blocked and nothing could be done. I knew that some of the people of the South of France were living on turnips and making soup from weeds in the hedges. In her anaemic and weakened state Elisabeth should be well and continually nourished. How could she survive such hardships?

As I could neither write to her nor nourish her, all I could do was to send my loving thoughts to her without interruption. Surely, sent with such force and concentration they MUST reach her? I shut myself up for hours in the little summer-house near the caravan, and there, on the surface of a deal store-cupboard at the foot of my camp bed (which I was now using because the summer-house had a fireplace), I painted Mademoiselle's courtyard with the door in the wall open to reveal her secret garden, and her slender form standing just inside. I used distempers and oil-paints and water-colours. I hadn't touched a brush since my schooldays, but now I painted like one possessed, sending my thoughts flying over the sea to Elisabeth all day and every day. At night as I lay in bed I still stared at my picture of her in her own lovely setting until at last I put out my candle, when I prayed for her and talked to her in the darkness.

One morning in March when I was doing my usual dreary treatment there came a knock at the door of the summer-house. I opened it and a village boy handed me a telegram. Cold and sick I opened it. It came from the British Embassy in Lisbon, and told me that Elisabeth was dangerously ill. I sent a wild cable imploring her to make every effort to get well because we needed her, and to assure her that she was surrounded by our love. The next day came another cable to tell me that the beloved *Mademoiselle* had died on February, the 25th — a month before. . . .

At moments like these action is a necessity. I rushed out into the woods, tortured by thoughts of her suffering and her loneliness — illustrated by my terribly vivid imagination. I did not know how I should be able to bear this blow. Walking blindly on I came out into a clearing of the woods flanked by a sloping bank covered with nodding golden daffodils, glorious in full sunlight. And amidst them I saw the lovely little head of Elisabeth — and she was LAUGHING FOR JOY.

CHAPTER
TWENTY-ONE

Work and Rest

Somehow I completed my programme in Devon, and then I was asked if I would organise Sussex for A.V.F. Our Devon chairman, one of the most brilliant and dynamic personalities I ever met, was perfectly capable of running the county without my aid, and I had already covered it by extensive propaganda and succeeded in rousing much enthusiasm for France. Sussex was virgin soil. I had hoped when my engagements in Devon were finished to have time to finish this poor interrupted book, but while I was needed to help France I must not relax. And so I consented to become chairman of the Sussex branch of A.V.F.

I hardly think that I could ever have returned to "Many Waters" with my Blackness had I not been told that Romulus, the red terror, now rarely left the Big House. He had had a blow on the head, probably from a passing car, for the red terrors wandered where they listed, and he was now blind in one eye, poor old man, and the sight of the other was going. I mourned for him because I love all dogs, and until the arrival of The Blackness and the jealous feud started we had been great friends. Now he was never allowed to go for walks unattended, and we were told that increasing age and infirmity had taken away all desire to descend the precipice and run wild in the woods with Rema as in the past. If I wired in my bit of valley at the back of the cottage so that Dominie could run in and out at will, it would be possible to return to our little home in the woods, and the long daily run in them would no longer be fraught with danger. And so we all came back, and I fell into my new work with the driven ferocity of the over-tired and unhappy, speaking at meetings all over the county and writing appeals until the small hours. My caravan companion was still living with me, for the work of transforming the Kennels into a bungalow was still in progress.

When it was finished and she took possession, a friend of John's niece, whom we all learned to call "Nanny" because of her genius for helping the helpless and tending the sick, came to "Many Waters" to look after Dominie and me. Though strongly approving all desire and effort to help the unfortunate, Nanny and I were continually at war over one subject — my health. She insisted that I must rest, and although I longed to relax I could never do this while there was so much misery in the world which I could lessen. So she did her best for me against what she considered hopeless odds. Poor old Nanny! The last straw was my final rash act, which must be described in a long chapter all to itself. With her massive chin jutting more prominently every day with disapproval, she yet threw herself into this mad adventure of mine, helping me in a thousand ways with her practical good sense and high intelligence

— helping me, bless her, to the point of exhaustion, but to a great triumph.

Our greatest bond was The Blackness, whom she adored and who loved her — and the delicious cakes she made. She allowed him to sit on a chair at the tea-table with his own tiny plate on which a special bun was always placed, and she also made two little private napkins for him with which we could hastily catch a shaming icicle of longing which *very* occasionally hung from his lips if we kept him waiting too long for his bun. On his birthday she even made him a special cake. She, too, had a bad attack of Cockeritis.

One lovely week-end of rest I had. "His Hugeness," introduced in my book *Trampled Lilies*, had always wanted me to know his married daughter, and had engineered a meeting for the three of us in — of all places — the *foyer* of The Strand Palace Hotel. Whenever he came to London he invariably took a room in some such place because, as he explained, besides being good and cheap, it gave him the opportunity of studying every type of human nature in the cosmopolitan mob he found there. Needless to say, he had long conversations with many.

I entered what is called "The Lounge," and saw him at once seated beside an extraordinarily beautiful woman. She looked like a goddess uncomfortably disguised in modern clothes. Her fashionable hat had been placed in a bored manner at the wrong angle on her lovely head. Her mass of dark hair was coiled on her neck and a wisp had escaped like a plume. Her great violet eyes under finely pencilled brows stared around her in utter

bewilderment. She had been translated from Atlantis into
— *this*!

His Hugeness spied me and uttered a welcoming "Ha
HA! There she is!" and introduced me to his daughter.
With an obvious effort she collected her thoughts, threw
back her lovely head and dazzled me with the smile
of an old friend, holding out both her hands with
sudden delightful spontaneity. Then she burst into
the most delicious chuckling laughter, opening her
mouth wide like a child and displaying a double row
of perfect teeth.

"Why are we *here*?" she exclaimed passionately. "This
seems to me like the ante-room of Hell." And then we
both laughed.

But it was here that my lovely week-end was planned.
She lived in an ancient house, once the property of monks
who had diverted the course of the river so that it squared
off the gardens and formed a flowing moat. Green lawns
led down to it and weeping willows fringed it. A place of
green peace and running water. His Hugeness had often
described it to me. Now I was to see it.

Those few days were an oasis in the desert of war. On
arrival I was greeted first by His Hugeness towering in
the doorway, standing with his arm around the shoulders
of his grandson, a blue-jacket of the Royal Navy, who
approached me with the same spontaneity as had his
mother, taking my hands in his and shaking them,
smiling into my eyes.

"Pretty good! Pretty good!" he said.

A great-grandchild was produced, a lovely golden
child with the firm fat legs and delicate skin of most

English children. Her naval uncle addressed her as "My Lover Queen" — a quaint and delightful name, I thought. I shall ever remember the picture of that child having her bath on the green lawn by the moat. Her uncle fetched a tin tub and several cans of water to fill it, and then baby Viola climbed in. Her lovely little body, as at intervals she climbed out of the bath and raced about the lawn, against a background of weeping willows and the scintillating water of the moat, was a thing too perfect ever to forget.

We sat under the shade of great trees, four generations of one family, all beautiful and loving one another very much; all hypersensitive and intelligent, and all, except baby Viola, doing interesting war work. The bluejacket, sitting cross-legged on the grass by my side diligently mending a pair of trousers to make them "tiddley," told me of various cruises. He described the bombing of Malta when he was in port. Three of the bluejackets had afterwards been sent round to collect lost or motherless babies. They repaired a shed and improvised a crèche, making cots from orange boxes, cutting up and sewing little sheets and blankets, mixing the babies' bottles, washing the infants and their nappies, giving the older children their orange juice and inventing games to amuse them. Once a week they sent for a doctor to examine all the children, but they refused all offers of help from the women of the island, and proudly ran the crèche themselves. Needless to say, it was spotless and kept in the most perfect order.

"He's a fine chap, the British A.B.," the narrator of this story assured me. "It always annoys me the bilge that is written about a sailor having a wife in every port. There is no more reliable and chivalrous type. I'd trust my sisters anywhere in the care of an A.B."

He spoke of their simplicity and intense kindness. One of the men in his ship found a canary with a broken leg. He made a splint for it, and another member of the crew netted a tiny scarlet silk hammock into which the crippled bird was loosely lashed until convalescent. This was suspended near a port-hole, and every sailor who passed it gently poked it with his finger to swing it and give the bird the illusion of flying. The ship's cat had a real bed, with a gay quilt and sheets and blankets hemmed by the sailors. So did they fill some of their off-duty hours at sea.

For the first time for weeks I slept beautifully in that place of peace and happiness. I was awakened by a tremendous voice singing grand opera somewhere in the house — my hostess enlivening the drudgery of housework as she violently swept the stairs. All through the war, although it gave her much extra work, she insisted upon using all the valuable china, silver and crystal, which she washed and cleaned herself. She said that when her children came home she wanted them always to find home exactly as it used to be, but she never put this extra work upon her depleted staff. "The children *do* so appreciate the lovely things, the darlings. And why, to save ourselves work, do we make life even drearier than it must be by using utility china and paper napkins? So sordid and sad."

I am rather a nib at cleaning silver, and during my visit I was allowed to be parlourmaid — a high honour to be trusted to handle precious things hitherto touched only by herself.

When I left, my host remarked: "Just our luck. We find the ideal parlourmaid, and then she leaves to better herself."

CHAPTER
TWENTY-TWO

Ups and Downs

There are fools, and hardy fools. I hope and think that I belong to the latter category, for all my life I seem to have been doing foolhardy deeds. Instead of seeking to avoid them with all the caution that *should* be in my composition, since I was made and born in Suffolk, even now I rush at them grey-curled (not yet bald-headed). Not until I'm so deeply involved that, if I turn tail and plunge back to serene safety I must inevitably let someone — probably many people — down with a flump, and also be accused of cowardice, does the awful truth flash into my stunned consciousness that once again I've been a fool. And very often FOOL spelt in capitals. It may be my Fighting Battye blood bequeathed to me by my gallant little mother, or perhaps that shadowy crusader ancestor who was my GREAT-great-great-great-great-great-great-grandfather, who urges me into these rash adventures, prods me to tilt quixotic lances, to defend hopeless causes and cases, and generally to attempt the apparently impossible.

Which brings me — at last — to that fatal fête — one of the most foolhardy acts of my life; for *only* a fool, and a hardy fool with more than a spice of daring and the gallant gambler in his veins, would attempt to organise a gigantic Fête Champêtre, entirely dependent on outdoor attractions, in this tricky climate of ours.

Lying awake one lovely night of June in my green studio room, smelling the fragrance of massed azaleas, staring at the starlit outlines of great beech trees on the edge of the rock cliffs seen from one of my windows, and hearing the murmur of many waters all around me, that dreadful Norman crusader suddenly whispered in my ear through the music of the waterfalls:

"WHAT a wonderful fête you could organise in this incomparable setting to help the French *Volontaires*!"

I bounced out of bed, startling The Blackness nearly out of his senses, and, to the accompaniment of his excited barks, ran into the small spare room next door, threw open its window overlooking the little lakes, soft and silvery in the mysterious June starlight, and leaned out. Dominie reared up on his hind legs and, placing two feathered front feet on the sill, leaned out too and sniffed the scented air.

Yes! What a setting! Drowsiness disappeared, my inflamed imagination began to smoulder and then to throw out sparks. Little boats lit by swaying Chinese lanterns drifting about the lakes. I had a nostalgic vision of the lake in the Bois de Boulogne in summers of the past. Ah! but no lanterns would be allowed in war-time, and nobody would or could come to a garden fête at night. No! Music, moonlight, romantic drifting among the water-lilies on the lake, dancing under the stars on the bowling-green of the Big House, a buffet supper in the rose garden — all these attractions must be ruled out by the black hand of war.

But much could be done, particularly for the children, in the daytime. If too many other galas and fêtes were not organised for Bank Holiday that would be the ideal day for mine. Surely my landlord, who was also the honorary treasurer for A.V.F., could be persuaded to back this enterprise and lend me his lovely estate for just one day? The bell in his clock tower far above on the cliff began to chime. Midnight — only twelve o'clock, and I must wait for hours and hours before I could know the fate of my fête! Sleep was now impossible, and how better could I employ those hours until to-morrow than by making lists? Immediately I saw the beloved *Mademoiselle*, perched on the edge of the great swimming-pool in her lovely secret garden, sleek little dark head bent over a writing-pad as she wrote lists of stores we should need and equipment we must take with us for a holiday in our tiny cottage on the rocks outside St. Tropez, in our coastguard station below Ramatuelle, or in our *bergerie* in the High Alps. Her wonderful comprehensive lists.

Pain gripped my heart as I remembered that never with her, on this earth, could I share such happiness again. If I went back to Provence I should find her château shuttered and empty. Could I bear to go back? Is it possible to begin life *again* on the extremely wrong side of fifty?

When someone we love with all that is best in us, someone who is part of ourselves, passes on into the Wider Life, the spiritually minded who wish to comfort remind us that those we love so intensely are still with us — always with us. Of course, we *know* this if we believe anything at all, but we, being human still and earth-bound, so long for the smell of that old coat of Harris tweed and that rank pipe we so often condemned and strove to cleanse; that gentle touch of a hand, the sound of that voice, the twinkle of eyes that could laugh in a stern face. A spirit-companion is the least cosy thing, and I, for one, could take no joy or comfort from the thought of it, so terribly human am I. Human — and imaginative. So that even when I have thought them to be near me I have swiftly said to myself: "You *want* them to be, and so you read their presence into signs and symbols which your imagination is telling you are their way of trying to communicate with you." Yet twice, in our little *domaine* near Grasse which he had loved so much, I did have proof positive that my John was still there with me, a year after he left it — and me — desolate.

I was writing in my tower room alone at night, and I wanted to refer to a passage in a collection of his lectures printed in book form and entitled *British Statesmen of the Great War*, a book long since out of print, but I knew there was a copy of it in his great *galerie* downstairs. He was so meticulous in his work that I must on no account misquote one word of his wonderful prose. I would go down and find the book. I went, and, search as I might, I could not discover it among the myriad books in those white book-shelves of his own special design which lined the walls of his *galerie*. Twice I toured the room, and failing still to find that book I gave up the search, and somewhat pettishly stumped up the marble staircase to my tower, resolving that I would skate round my difficulty and make a vague reference to what John had said. With a weary sigh I sat down in my writing-chair and picked up my pencil. And then it was as though strong arms gently but very firmly raised me from the chair, and strong hands upon my shoulders propelled me to the door of the room and down the staircase once again to the *galerie* on the ground floor. I went reluctantly, even sulkily, like a child compelled to do something it doesn't want to do. I was really *very* cross as I switched on my electric torch and, walking over to the bookcase, swung the light almost defiantly upon the books before me. The little circle of brilliant light shone at once upon *British Statesmen of the Great War*.

That *did* astonish me. And yet, when I thought of it afterwards, an historian as conscientious as John (I have seen him destroy three hundred pages of manuscript, the work of months, because in his researches he had discovered one small fact which changed the aspect of a military campaign which must now be re-written) would never allow an untrained amateur like me perhaps to misquote or misinterpret one sentence that he had written after much careful thought, weighing of evidence and sifting of facts. Because of this passion for truth his *History of the British Army* will live for all time as a classic.

The other evidence of his near presence was even more remarkable. He had published a series of articles on military subjects and personalities which, in book form, he called *Following the Drum*. He intended to publish a second book containing a further collection, and he had this ready for his publisher when he fell ill. "We'll publish it next year," he said to me, "and you,

Sweetheart, must find a 'popular' title with a military sound like the first."

I had to do this after he left me, and the obvious and only title then was *The Last Post*. And because, after the Last Post there must be silence, it was imperative that I should include in that collection the best of his lectures on military subjects. Philip Guedalla helped me with this selection, and promised to correct the proofs of the book when it was published, since the campaigns described could not be as familiar to me as to him. For years he had sat at John's feet, and John had helped him with his *Peninsular War*. He asked me to "accept the services of a very willing volunteer," and I was both grateful and thankful.

Soon after I had despatched the manuscript to Mr. Blackwood I had to go to Paris for a long torture treatment. On my return I found a tremendous pile of proofs lying on John's desk, and also a letter from Philip Guedalla regretting very sadly that *his* publisher was demanding the finished manuscript of his forthcoming book, *The Hundred Days*, which meant that he could not possibly now undertake the correction of John's proofs. But he would be most happy and honoured if I would allow him to write a short preface to the book.

Well, as John so often said, there it was. I must strive to make the best of that job alone, and I really didn't see how I could help making a mess of it, since many of the chapters dealt with little-known campaigns, and my knowledge of military history is distinctly limited.

However, when I've got to do a difficult or unpleasant thing I must always tackle it at once. So I dismissed my little fat Emilia to her bed, squared my shoulders, and sat down before that great desk of John's in his dim *galerie* and opened that formidable packet of proofs. I remember saying aloud as I did so: "Darling! You MUST help me. I'm no military historian — only your very weary woman." Then I turned over the first page of proof, and my eyes were immediately confronted by the entirely (to me) unknown and unpronounceable name of some place in India. Ohhhhhhhhh . . . ! Its spelling must, of course, be verified. And I should doubtless — eventually — find that name on one of the thousands of pages of the thirteen fat red volumes of John's *History of the British Army*. As I hadn't the faintest idea in which of those volumes to search for the account of that particular campaign, it didn't matter at all which volume I consulted first. So I took one at random, opened it just anyhow, and there before me was the name of that outlandish place. I am glad that in my amazement I did not afterwards forget to say: "Oh, *thank* you, beloved."

He corrected his own proofs. I had no trouble at all. Always I found immediately the name or place I sought, though always opening one or other of those red volumes seemingly at random.

Of course, so great an historian would not allow his wife who, though ignorant, was so intensely proud of his work and of him, to make a mess of it. I might have known that. Indeed, I *must* have known it subconsciously, or why did I appeal thus to him before I began my search?

These are the wonderful and mysterious things that sometimes come to help us, and the remembrance of them in those terrible "small hours" of every morning, when vitality is at its lowest, one's feet are cold and one's tumpkin empty, can greatly comfort. So — think on these things when the symptoms appear.

The hours were still small when the thought of Elisabeth's disappearance from this earth completely punctured my enthusiasm for the garden fête. But — it was a very good idea, which, if I could pump up enough energy and enthusiasm to develop into a reality, might prove a very fruitful source of help for those pathetic and so gallant *poilus* who had rallied to the call of Général de Gaulle to fight on with their allies.

Did I — or I did *imagine* that I heard Elisabeth whisper:

"*Go on*, Pegs! *Do* it. A wonderful idea."

Masters of form in prose-writing will doubtless long ago have shut this book (if it ever becomes a book) with an irritable bang, probably saying: "Why can't the woman stick to her theme? She leads us to think that she's going to describe a Bank Holiday fête, and then meanders away from her subject to describe sensations, imaginings, visions — so like a woman." Yes, I admit that I am all woman, and that my greatest difficulty is complete concentration, although I lived for twenty years with a man who could and did fully use the sixty seconds of each minute, and once completed the most difficult chapter of his great *History* while the woman he loved more than his *History* was undergoing an operation upstairs. While he was working he was blind, deaf and dumb; whereas I have never yet succeeded in keeping my attention firmly fixed — even through the Litany — my test of concentration. I resolve each time NOT to be so miserable a sinner, and to pray like a steam engine for every person or thing one asks a patient God to save or to protect in that interminable category, but every time that imagination of mine upsets the apple-cart — I mean the sequence. The furthest that I ever got by sweating effort is to, "That it may please Thee to preserve all that travel by land or by water, all women labouring of child. . . ." Then I started dreaming of little sea voyages with John, and of every friend of mine about to have a baby — and suddenly the voice of the priest begins to intone, "Our Father," and I find I have missed five clauses and the frantic petitions that follow them. Defeated again. Since the war, *if* I get beyond "From all evil and mischief," I never progress further than ". . . from plague, pestilence and *famine* . . ." and after that my mind, heart and soul are suffering with the starving peoples of Europe.

When I am writing, if I look up and my eyes fall upon a tiny vase of early white violets standing before Mummie's picture, my mind flies back over the years, and once again I am finding the first violets for her in our wild rectory garden under the three graceful silver birches bordering the drive. Then, of course, I must wander on, down over the grass slopes to the place where thousands of primroses grew under the dappled shade of great trees and on to the wilderness — where I get hopelessly lost amid a tangle of budding undergrowth — and lovelier memories. The note of a bird will call away my spirit — a lark transports me to the flower-starred mountains of the High Alps and the fresh fragrance of snow peaks and glaciers. And in every scene the personalities of those I shall love for ever are in the foreground, and things they

said or did rush into my lonely mind to comfort me. I
know that I am far from unique in this, and that is why
my readers bear with my curious bubbling conversation.
Probably they have experienced like things, but perhaps
have not found the same consolation in them because
they did not look deep enough, or dismissed those things
as vain imaginings because they wanted to believe them.
And so even my irrelevances may help them. I pray they
may, and I pray the purists to forgive me.

And now I really will return to that fatal fête!

The next day, when my landlord descended the
precipice for a little evening talk, I laid my scheme
before him. He looked a bit startled at first, for in the
past he had suffered much from London trippers who,
when allowed to visit these lovely grounds, rewarded him
by throwing paper bags and banana skins (this was very
long ago — the fruit dates it) into his lakes, and tearing
down blossoming branches to take home with them. Since
when — padlocks and forbidding notice boards. The pity
of it, for always the innocent suffer for the guilty, and
this place is one of the prides of Sussex.

However, when I promised to have guardians at the
gates, and reminded him that there would be A.V.F.
helpers everywhere, he soon gave his permission, and
began with young enthusiasm to see visions of his own.
He suggested opening the proceedings by an invitation
luncheon to be given by himself, if I would send out
the invitations, act as hostess, since I was chairman of
the Sussex Central Committee of A.V.F., and see to the
catering. The Big House was still occupied by babies
from London, and his mother and he were still tucked

into tiny lodges on the estate. So all their possessions — silver, glass, china, linen — were packed away in the basement of their home, and these things must, therefore, be hired.

Suddenly he paused — Bank Holiday! How to feed the multitude? It must be upon unrationed food. Fish was indicated — lobsters, salmon — but these would have to be bought on Saturday and kept till Monday. Were there enough Frigidaires in Sussex to house a sufficiency of fish . . . ? I simply would not listen to the practical objections of a business man. There WOULD be fish enough to feed the multitude, as there was on another seemingly hopelessly-hungry occasion.

My landlord is young, rich and resourceful. He must just bend his clever brain to the food problem when the moment came, for this would be *his* only problem (I hoped) on the Great Day, whereas I began dimly to realise that mine would be many.

We discussed weather possibilities; August Bank Holiday could be very wet indeed, and if it rained, the al fresco luncheon party in the rose garden would be washed out. In that awful case, could the L.C.C. babies be shut away somewhere in the Big House and its larger lower rooms utilised? Yes — doubtfully — but they had been stripped of everything beautiful; linoleum covered the parquet, rocking horses must be stabled elsewhere, fifty little enamel pots removed from the cloak-room, and so on. The luncheon party would degenerate into a kind of school treat. No! it MUST be out of doors. A marquee on the bowling green? Tent pegs for ever ruin turf. No! that luncheon must be held in the paved rose garden, and it was up to *le bon Dieu* to give us a fine day for so good a cause. He most certainly WOULD.

Permission to use these glorious grounds gained. An invitation luncheon promised, and a spark of enthusiasm faintly smouldering in him who would confer these benefits. Not a bad prelude to a great adventure. At any rate I should have a powerful ally to back my mad enterprise.

Next — ATTRACTIONS! Sports and pony rides for the children, and voyages in a rowing boat at so much a tour of the lowest and largest of the lakes. Bathing for the adolescent, perhaps even al fresco dancing, archery, games of skill. A concert or play to amuse their elders; a boxing match to enthral the lads of the village, and various stalls of flowers, garden produce and preserves, "fancy" goods for the benefit of their mammas — and the French — and a picnic tea outside "Many Waters," from whence gallons of tea must spout to refresh the thirsty multitude — for of course the weather would be hot and sunny for MY fête and hundreds of people would come.

"But you can't get hundreds of chairs and tables down the precipice and then up again," objected some practical person.

"Chairs!" I ejaculated scornfully. "Let the Nobs on the upper terraces around the Big House sit on the few chairs there'll be. *My* friends will *prefer* sitting on the grass."

"And if it rains beforehand?" persisted that maddening person.

"It WON'T rain," I asserted stoutly, rolling a defiant eye at the heavens which at that moment were watering us copiously, "but I'll get some tarpaulins to console you."

These vague ideas must now be crystallised into a practical programme. Helpers must be found to organise the children's sports, but that was easily arranged, for the head teacher of the home for babies in the Big House very kindly undertook to do this, helped by her assistants. Various children of the neighbourhood who possessed ponies volunteered to ride them over and then to walk them around the lakes with the children of the village astride; others offered to row cargoes of children around the lake and be responsible for their safe — and dry — return. The bathing would be easy. On my posters I would announce that this sport was only for swimmers, who must bring their costumes. They could undress in the tunnels of rhododendrons, which must be marked WOMEN — MEN (as LADIES and GENTLEMEN, though more popularly polite, might be misunderstood). Just as I had planned all this my landlord appeared to warn me that there were dangerous hidden rocks in that lake, and so diving must be forbidden. "You must put up printed warnings," he insisted, "saying DIVING DANGEROUS: HIDDEN ROCKS — and you'd better get some good swimmers to hang around and some first-aid people or nurses in case of cramp or accidents." I felt my inside slowly turning over as my imagination pictured these horrors, and I resolved to follow his advice.

The village policeman and other sportsmen promised to arrange a boxing match, and soon afterwards I was informed that two experienced boxers had been found in the ranks of a regiment quartered in a neighbouring village, and had willingly agreed to give an exhibition of their horrible skill for the delectation of the male population of the village.

A fabulously rich lady promised to produce "London artists" for an entertainment. She would arrange it all and I had nothing to do but print ENTERTAINMENT on my programme. How lovely — and what a relief! Then, if a shower should fall in the afternoon, people could listen to beautiful music or be entertained in some manner — indoors — with the babies. But a "highbrow" concert, if this proved to be the kind of entertainment provided, would not amuse the usual Bank Holiday crowd, and music of some popular kind we must have all the afternoon to hearten the proceedings. A fête without music is naught.

A regimental band! The very thing. And with soldiers swarming the neighbourhood surely I could find brass instruments enough and soldierly lungs strong enough to blow blasts of melody loud enough to drown the sound of any siren that might chance to wail in the distance? At once I started my search for a band — more difficult than one would imagine, for the haunts of regiments were carefully hidden, and no civilian could be given the telephone number of any regimental headquarters. However, by subtlety and discreet enquiry I discovered a Scottish regiment whose officers promised to provide pipers. Wonderful! I had a vision of swinging kilts and in imagination heard the skirl and wail of bagpipes as the pipers marched about in the woods and round the lakes. How thrilled the people would be!

Climbing precipices while with bursting lungs you inflate bagpipes must surely exhaust even the stoutest Scot, and so I decided also to hire the local electrician, who often provided dance music from an electric gramophone relayed through loud-speakers. These could be hung in the trees and surely — surely — enough wire could be found to span the precipice down to the lakes and "Many Waters," where the multitude would be eating their picnic tea? I consulted the electrician, and he made light of all difficulties. I remembered to ask him if his apparatus would work on the voltage of the Big House, and suggested that he should verify this at an early date. He laughed at my anxiety, assuring me that he had made various electric installations in and about that property, and knew all about the voltage, and so forth. Calmed, I left him to it, for I had plenty to occupy me.

I had to cope with the enthusiasm of my landlord which now waxed hot. Every evening when he returned from the City he descended the precipice with fresh names to be included on the list of those to be invited to his luncheon party. At first only a select few were to be invited — perhaps twenty-five. By the end of the first week there were fifty names on our list, which finally swole (is that a word? I don't think so, but it's expressive) to over a hundred.

Having sent out the invitations for the luncheon and billed "Picnic Tea" on the posters, the food agony began. My landlord had relied upon things outside the ration, but every purveyor of fish seemed to have long ago promised his coming supply to other Bank Holiday beanos, and would not commit himself further. There remained chickens as a possibility — but in August poultry farmers can generally spare only a few "boilers," their tender spring chickens having been devoured long since. My landlord was in despair. And when I was informed that I could not be allowed extra milk for the picnic teas, even for so deserving a cause, I nearly gave up the ghost, for posters promising that picnic tea at one shilling a head were already plastered everywhere. At night I lay awake and agonised, having, fruitlessly bombarded adamantine officials all day, but suddenly one night I startled my Blackness from his slumber with the loud cry of "GOATS!" Instantly he sprang, barking, from his basket, and searched for them in every corner of the room. I calmed him. Goats' milk was not rationed. WHO among my friends and acquaintance kept goats? An inspiration sent straight from the land flowing with milk and honey. Oh yes! and HONEY (likewise unrationed). Where could I find honey for the children's sandwiches? Blessing the fact that I was born into a clerical family, I then fell asleep.

Helpers I did not lack; the only trouble was that although they would spare me that one precious day, and on it devote all their energies, all of them were so occupied and overworked in their efforts to win the war by other means that not one of them could come to me beforehand to be shown the position of his stall or game of chance or refreshment tent, and on an estate so large, with so many entrance gates, I foresaw difficulties — perhaps chaos ahead. The gardeners willingly offered to guard the various gates and sell tickets, and I arranged for a band of school children to act as "runners," wear tricolour cockades, and lead helpers and public to the various amusements. These children I carefully instructed and drilled beforehand, and they were to be stationed at the various entrance gates both above and below the precipice.

Crockery and cutlery I succeeded in hiring, on condition that it was fetched — always from afar. I was promised a lorry to do the journeys, which at the same time could collect garden chairs from various houses, flags and bunting from Chailey, urns and a dart-board from the canteen in the village (on condition that they were returned in good time for the soldiers' use that same evening).

I had implored my White Lady, a great artist in the planning and arrangement of flowers and food, to be responsible for the luncheon menu — if her son succeeded in finding any food — and she became as distracted as he. Her marvellous cook would dress and mayonnaise the lobsters and salmon and transform the chickens into birds of paradise (IF they could be found), albeit she had only an electric ring, a tiny kitchen stove and an oil lamp in the little lodge. Madame la Mère still led a cramped existence, but I had sampled gastronomic miracles prepared by the wonderful Madge in her toy lodge, and I had no fears for that "Invitation Luncheon" IF food could be produced from somewhere for her to cook and beautify. In any case, even if we were reduced to a variety of sandwiches and fruit salads from the estate, I did not see how people who were to pay nothing for their food could complain. If they felt a bit empty afterwards, they could feast on the beauty around them, for in all

England I doubted if they could find a lovelier setting for their mastication.

Drinks! Wine scarce and prohibitive in price — a cask of cider would be the very thing. Heartened once more, my gallant landlord returned to ransack London for drinks and delicacies, for if he undertook to do a thing, it must be done well. A beloved friend of mine offered to provide the cakes, rolls and biscuits for my teas, and a gigantic "Guess its weight" cake — always a popular competition. These would come from Brighton, but must be met at the station and conveyed six and a half miles to "Many Waters" — another little transport problem, for many of my helpers had to be fetched too. My little secretary for A.V.F. had a car, and I asked two girl drivers to run a taxi service with her car and the little Grey Pigeon. Oh, we should manage somehow!

As time went on, growing anxious because I had heard nothing from the lady who had promised to provide an entertainment, I sent her a reply-paid telegram asking if a piano would be required. Silence for two days, and then came the answer: "Artist unable to come."

ARTIST! In the singular. Very singular — not to say shattering. It was raining dismally when I got that reply, and the same evening I was given a message telling me that the regiment containing my army boxers had vanished in the night. Foolishly I had forgotten that in war-time this might easily happen. Probably my pipers would disappear in like manner — but at any rate I should always have the loud-speaker music provided by the electrician. Another message was brought to me — from him — he was terribly sorry, but to his shame he had discovered that the voltage of the Big House was not powerful enough for his musical apparatus. How he could possibly have forgotten the voltage he did not know, because he had so often done jobs there — and so on. Frantically I pounded up the precipice and telephoned to him. Music MUST be provided — somehow — I had relied on him, and I KNEW that he wouldn't let me down. Think of the disappointment of those hundreds of people, I babbled. I was told that the only hope was to find two 12-volt car batteries to reinforce the existing line.

Hours I spent at that telephone ringing up every electrician and garage in the neighbourhood. One 12-volt battery was almost impossible to find — and I wanted two. In despair I rang up Richard Hillary's Mr. Baker, who, since I first met him, had solved many of my problems, generally achieving the impossible. He at once gave me the name of a friend of his who sold tyres and might be able to find the batteries. Yes, I could ring him at his private house. I did — and, although he possessed none, he thought he could find me two in a few days. I told him the fête was almost upon us, and I mingled gratitude with urgent prayers, and had to leave it at that.

In the evening my landlord visited me, and looked very glum when I broke all this bad news to him. All my "attractions" fading away.

"We've got to have an auction," he suddenly exclaimed. Your pony rides and bathing and games and one-shilling teas and cheap entrance tickets won't bring in enough to pay for your printing and expenses.

You must have an auction. Ask all our friends to bring something to be auctioned — drinks, fruit, bibelots, books — anything — and find a clever and amusing auctioneer — an actor or music hall artist. An auction will bring in money. We can have it after luncheon, before the general public are admitted at two-thirty p.m."

Again I climbed the precipice and sent an SOS to my secretary, who leaped into her car and joined me within the hour. Together we wrote letters and addressed envelopes. It would be a jumpy business, this auction, because at such short notice we shouldn't have time to learn what — if anything — our friends would or could supply to be auctioned, and I must engage an auctioneer to auction objects which might not exist. Ah! la la! as the French say. But eventually I did find a brave man willing to take the risk.

When I had fixed Bank Holiday for my fête I had taken pains to find out that it would collide with no other fête; for not only did I crave a large attendance, but always have I deplored overlapping of effort in the cause of humanity. At that moment no one contemplated giving a fête, and we were looked upon as public benefactors because we were supplying amusements for children who could then have very few. But the moment the posters appeared every one seemed to catch my idea, and a positive rash of posters announcing rival fêtes in the surrounding towns and villages appeared in the windows of shops and village halls. Every day someone or other depressed me further with news of yet another glorious day of entertainment offered to the public for the fee of one shilling, in aid of . . .

The most formidable from my point of view were, first, a fête to be given by the Army (in aid of the local Red Cross Hospitals) in our largest town. A tank of silver cardboard was built on the framework of an army lorry, and, filled with wounded men in hospital blue and khaki figures with bugles, blundered and bugled its way through the streets advertising the attractions to be offered. At intervals it stopped so that the public might read the proffered programme, and to allow war-minded little boys to finger the ugly noses of guns which protruded through the cardboard armour plating. With eyes on stalks I read BAND OF SCOTTISH PIPERS. . . . My pipers? Agony.

I hurried home to telephone to the officer who had promised them to me. Yes, it was too true. Superior officers not knowing of — or perhaps ignoring the promise of pipers made to me by this captain — had offered the band to enhance the attractions of the Army fête. I knew that our hospitals must and should take priority over any other cause, but this did not lessen my despair. To console me the captain promised to do his best to spare me perhaps *two* pipers, but he could make no certain statement.

The second formidable rival was a pony gymkhana in a neighbouring village to which, of course, all the children who had promised to lend me the services of themselves and their ponies would long to go — and how could I have the heart to prevent them?

I felt exactly like a tyre with a slow puncture, daily losing air.

No entertainment.

No boxing match.

Doubtful electrical music.

An auctioneer achieved, but no certainty of having anything to auction.

Problematical pipers.

Ye gods and little fishes! And would my landlord be able to find big fishes for his luncheon party?

Facing facts squarely in the night watches I realised that all I had left in the way of attractions depended entirely upon good weather. Given a fine day, tired people might prefer to wander in the grounds of a lovely private property to the hectic amusements provided by a fête in the square of a town. Parents I hoped, would feel that with the ever-present possibility of air raids their children would be safer where woods and rocks provided cover. BUT — torrential rain would inevitably wash away all my attractions, for who would linger in dripping woods or saunter or ride ponies over sodden turf surrounding muddied rain-swollen lakes? Who would have the courage to plunge and disport themselves in such waters? Who recline upon wet grass and enjoy a picnic tea outside "Many Waters" while much water trickled down their necks? The answer was, of course, NO ONE.

Well, the Providence which gives us more than we ask or think gave me a heat wave for the fête. My few attractions were safe, but my already quaking spirit quailed at the prospect of sweating all day up and down that precipice; for luncheon and stalls and sports were to be held on the upper terraces round the Big House, on the tennis courts and in the paddock. And all those were a quarter of a mile from the lakes and woods below, where the pony rides and aquatic sports and picnic tea would take place — and the temperature was over 80 degrees in the shade. In the late fifties one's legs prance less easily than in youth; muscles ache as one climbs steeply; one's interior seems to be suspended upon an ever-slackening string; one's heart beats in one's nose, and conversation, if any, is made in gasps. Humiliated and infuriated by the approaching anti-climax of AGE, one pauses at intervals pretending to absorb the beauties of the surrounding scene, but in reality to inflate one's bellows, hoping that the companion (if younger) will not notice one's distress.

All this happened to me each time I scaled the precipice. My one consolation was that I should at any rate keep my streamline.

THE DAY dawned, a soft mist shrouding the lakes and the sun, which gave promise of blazing all day upon our festivities — and on us. As the grounds were not to be open to the public till half-past two, and the guests for luncheon were not invited until twelve-forty-five, we had all the morning in which to put up flags and bunting and see to our final arrangements. Therefore I put on cool pale-green linen trousers, a flowered overall and battered South of France shady hat, and climbed the precipice for the first time that day. My gallant secretary was already at work, her little face flushed, her fair curls on end, her blue eyes bright with anxiety, her spindle legs twinkling all over the place — a whirlwind of activity, never losing her temper however many people hurled questions at her at the same time. She had a sweet but sometimes deprecatory smile for them all, and always a soothing and satisfying answer delivered in her small gentle voice.

We embraced, and then exchanged a humorous glance. Only we two, who had shared the preliminary agonies, the hopes so often shattered, the awful uncertainties, could realise the pitfalls, the hurdles, perhaps the blank walls that still lay ahead of us. Perhaps our helpers would fail to materialise as had the promised gift lorry which was to have collected crockery and chairs on the previous day. We had found a slow but sturdy horse and a small cart to fetch local things, and had bribed a coal merchant to send his lorry for those at a distance. My little Grey Pigeon had flown to the station to pick up buns and cakes from the Brighton train, but we were very doubtful about the human element.

I started to climb walls, and was festooning them with gaily coloured pennants when suddenly from behind me a voice said: "We are quite sure that you are '*Madame.*' This can only be *Madame* of *Perfume from Provence*? We imagined you to look exactly like that."

Trousered, perched on a wall entangled in roses and bunting, grubby scratched hands, grey curls damp with heat escaping from under the oldest and most faded hat in the world, and probably a smut or a grass stain on the nose. A thoroughly dignified position and costume in which to be caught. Below me stood a naval commander and, I imagined, his wife and family, all laughing up at me.

"Lady Fortescue — for surely you *are* Lady Fortescue —"

"Yes, I *am* that unfortunate woman," I replied.

"We came early in case we could help in some way. We've many links with France. It's the greatest cheek to come before you're invited — but it's such a heavenly day — and one doesn't often get a chance of getting inside a place like this."

"Did you buy your entrance tickets?" I asked severely.

"No, because there was no one to buy them from," he riposted, with truth, because of course, not anticipating an early invasion like this, I had arranged for the Guardians of the Gates to be in their places only half an hour before the grounds were opened to the public. He produced five shillings, and I sent the family away to picnic in the woods, saying that I was past human aid and had better be left alone.

Thenceforth a stream of trippers filtered across the lawns, mostly carrying large picnic baskets or paper bags.

"'Ere's our money, dear. We couldn't find no one ter give it to. Well — we know we're a bit *early* (it was then ten o'clock), but such a luvverly day, and as we've come all the way from Brighton — or Worthing — or Little'ampton — or Bognor — we thought we'd bring our food an' mike a day of it."

Heaven alone knows how many hundreds of people entered those spacious grounds by distant gates unperceived by us and so escaped paying entrance fees.

I was still in an agony of suspense about my electrical music when, accompanied by a kind man, I descended the precipice to place round the lakes the warning notices

I had had printed. I was standing on a stepping-stone fixing DIVING DANGEROUS to a post, when suddenly I nearly disobeyed my own warnings as a loud, raucous voice accosted me deafeningly from the region of the Big House a quarter of a mile away, followed by a blatant blast of jazz music. Regaining my balance I nearly fell into the sympathetic arms of my helper. Two 12-volt car batteries had miraculously been found! Electrical music was now braying from loud-speakers all over the estate. Saved!

As chairman of the Sussex Branch of *Amis des Volontaires Français* I was to be the hostess for the luncheon, and must clean off the marks of toil and array myself suitably to receive the important personages who were coming from London to grace my fête with their presence. The French Ambassador, loved and respected by all, had died suddenly a few days before as a result of the hardships and privations he had suffered as a Resistant. He would be replaced by the Acting Ambassador, Monsieur Paris, and General Sicé, *Délégué Militaire* of the *Croix Rouge Française*, would accompany him, together with some of our Foreign Office officials who occupied themselves with French affairs. I ought, therefore, to wear the uniform *Mademoiselle* and I wore while working with the French Army. Heavy cloth tunic and skirt of dark blue with a Chasseur Alpin beret. I had discussed the matter of clothes with my landlord, and he had begged me to wear the lightest and most feminine attire on such a purely secular occasion — *and* a shady hat.

"You'll faint if you wear that heavy uniform in this heat," he had said, loosening his collar and mopping his face, and, agreeing with him, I intended to follow his advice. He had slid down the precipice on Saturday night to apprise me of the fact that all the purveyors of fish who had assured him of the impossibility of supplying him with any for Bank Holiday had not only succeeded but exceeded his demands. He had travelled down from London chaperoning thirty lively lobsters, two gigantic but, happily for him, somnolent salmon and, rarity of rarities, a complete *saumon fumé* from Scandinavia. His clever mother had somehow caught six fat chickens; someone else had sacrificed an American ham and two enormous ox tongues; and the cask of cider — a huge cask — had arrived bubbling and singing — a most heady beverage.

"We've enough food now for three hundred people," he sighed wearily. "You'll have to have an overflow buffet down here and sell what is left over to the multitude. I've been flying around the country with fish begging the hospitality of all the Frigidaires of our neighbours. We can't house more than two huge lobsters and half a salmon in ours."

I laughed weakly.

He had arranged that the earliest of the important personages to arrive from London should be received in his own bachelor lodge. He could provide apéritifs for a chosen few, and the rest of the guests must be consoled with cider cup later. Ladies who wished to leave wraps and impedimenta and to powder their noses could use the upstair rooms of the Big House, since the L.C.C. babies would be caged on the ground floor. My secretary was deputed by him to aid him with the reception and unobtrusive selection of the guests on their arrival, while I was asked to await them a quarter of an hour later, posed on the stone steps of the rose garden under the great flags of France and England.

Afterwards I heard that my poor little overworked secretary, detained here by a gardener unable to fix a tottering flag, and there by other gardeners demanding their rolls of admission tickets and bags of small change; questioned by the electrician as to when he should start playing popular music, what tunes and for how long intervals; by a "loan" butler, who asked where wine-glasses could be found; by the cockaded school children, who had already forgotten where each was to stand, had barely time to rush away, tear off her dusty garments, throw on her gala attire and pound back to the Big House, where she found my frantic landlord almost submerged by a seething sea of invited — and uninvited — guests who, seeing a few people enter his lodge, followed like sheep till there was no room to move in the tiny rooms. Important and unimportant persons were hopelessly mixed; the few wine-glasses placed for the French officials from London seemed reproachfully inadequate, and when he fled to the cellars of the Big House in search of more sherry, he found on his return a mob of lovely ladies powdering their noses in the private bathroom of his lodge. Naturally he could not eject them or explain that the use of it was intended for men only.

I missed all this, posed in magnificent boredom under my flags, my only amusement being to watch members of the public peering into the roped-off rose garden and excitedly pointing out to each other delicacies on the buffet, beautifully arranged by my landlord's mother and her wonderful Madge, food such as they had not seen since before the war.

"Ohhhhh! Smoked salmon; actually smoked salmon!"

"My dear — LOBSTERS — millions of them!" and so on.

One hungry lady actually crawled under the rope barrier and, approaching the table, chose what she would like to eat (a sample of everything, I was told afterwards), and asked one of the attendants to reserve her this and that.

Presently Monsieur and Madame Paris and General Sicé, with representatives of our Foreign Office, appeared on the bowling green below the rose garden, escorted by my landlord laden like a pack-mule with baskets of fruit, bottles of wine and many odd parcels, followed by my secretary, her frail form hung with flowers, pictures, cushions and her little arms piled high with books.

Gifts for my auction! For the moment I had forgotten the auction! We had to fetch the auctioneer from the rival Army fête, where he was to function first, six miles away. Thank heaven he would at least have something to auc.

Luncheon was a scrum. It was really intended to be a case of "either — or"; you could have *either* fresh salmon *or* smoked salmon *or* lobster, but people starved of all luxury through those dreary war years took all three. How they found room afterwards for chicken, ham, tongue and salads of all kinds, including fruit salads and luscious peaches, passed my comprehension.

The heat was tropical, and I could scarcely swallow one mouthful of chicken, which was hardly in my mouth when a messenger asked for another roll of one thousand tickets for the main gate.

It seemed an incredibly short time before the buffet was bare. Yes, BARE. My landlord need have had no fears of a surplus. His munificence had been appreciated. The fame of his superb luncheon formed the one topic of conversation in the county of Sussex for a week. Fortunately, as I was afterwards told, that cask of heady cider was also empty — fortunately, because the fermenting fluid apparently went to the heads of bidders who offered fantastic prices when the auction began. I heard a first bid of fifteen pounds for a bottle of brandy, and my knees nearly gave way; but just at that moment I was called away to distribute the sports prizes to the children on the tennis courts, so that I did not hear a bid of £250 for a lovely little Jersey heifer anchored to a tree in the orchard, which was eventually bought back by the generous donor. It was led back home in triumph by the almost tearful cowman, who adored it, to the strains of strange diabolical squawks and squeals which proved to emanate from the bagpipes of two Scots pipers marching, unregarded, up and down the bowling green. This they did for five minutes, then vanished to the cover of trees (so I was told) and drank beer. Wise men.

Prizes given away, I galloped down the precipice to receive my guests for the picnic tea at 4 p.m., only to find the last urn squeezed dry and every roll, bun, sandwich and cake devoured. Flushed helpers from the Women's

Institute told me that they had started giving teas at half-past two, and had already served three hundred people!

"And look at that awful, hopeful queue half-way down to the lakes! We've only a loaf and some lettuce leaves left," exclaimed the lady in charge desperately. "I ought not to have been so generous to first-comers, but it was so lovely to give them a real blow-out for one shilling after all these days of rationing."

"Give them watery tea and lettuce sandwiches for twopence," I suggested. "Better than nothing," and I went among the people apologising. Those who had fed lay stretched and replete upon the grass, while The Blackness, swollen with cake, and with his collar adorned by an enormous tricolour bow to show that he was a Fighting Frenchman, towed the adorer to whom I had confided him for the afternoon amid the groups of people, in search of more crumbs and compliments.

No sirens disturbed us; young people swam in the cool waters of the lake, the boat was laden with laughing children, and the three ponies *not* competing in that rival gymkhana did overtime carrying others on their backs. Dear General Sicé and his wife had wandered down to have a word with me alone. Perhaps, for a moment, I might sit down and rest with them. But oh, no. I might not. The village policeman approached me with ponderous strides. A lady had succumbed to the heat and was in a fainting condition on the top terrace (it *would* be the top terrace). Had her Ladyship by any chance any smelling salts? She had. She would come at once. Dizzily I climbed the precipice again, and was led to the only *chaise-longue*, where a woman who looked to me in perfect health lay, with eyes closed, surrounded by anxious males fanning her and moistening her brow with elaborate silk handkerchiefs. I envied her. How lovely to lie on the only *chaise-longue* in a bower of roses fanned and moistened by kind young men.

A woman separated herself from the surrounding crowd!

"I am a nurse. Can I do anything?"

She bent over the prostrate form and put her finger on the languid wrist. Then she looked secretly at me. *Did* she wink? At any rate she did something with one eye, then said — to reassure the public — "She'll be all right. It's all over now. Just give her air and let her lie quietly there." Aside, in a whisper to me, "Shamming — pulse strong — nothing whatever wrong with her."

As I had thought. Wise woman. Clever woman.

The day wore on. People began to trickle away to catch buses, though the locals lingered. At last I could relax for a few moments and, in the peace of my studio room of "Many Waters," offer thanks and cigarettes to helpers who had worked so hard, and receive money boxes from stall-holders and others.

Apparently the people who had promised to supervise stalls and games *did* turn up in the end, though not at the appointed hour nor in the appointed place, but while I was hostessing they had found something to do, and had done it, as their heavy money boxes proved. My secretary appeared excitedly to announce that, with the money in our boxes, we had cleared over £700 that afternoon.

AMAZING!

Everything had seemed to me chaotic; everything I had tried to organise had broken down. Even my "runners" — the cockaded village children who were to act as guides — had failed me, and I never saw one of them during the whole afternoon. My secretary and I had done the running while those children sported, rode ponies and rowed on the lake. So that this unprecedented success was nothing short of miraculous. I thanked my helpers from a full heart, and also *le bon Dieu*, who had mercifully provided wonderful weather.

When every one had gone and I emerged from my studio to go downstairs for supper old Nanny told me that, half an hour before, she had seen a tall, foreign-looking gentleman, accompanied by a smartly dressed lady, climbing the stairs towards my studio. The front door had been left open all day. She had shooed them down again, saying that I was engaged and couldn't be disturbed.

"He didn't give his name? I wonder who he was?" I said wearily.

After supper there was still one last climb up that awful precipice which must be made. I could not sleep until I had thanked my sweet little secretary for her unselfish and untiring aid. Without her constant help I should have been lost indeed. To be near me she had arranged to stay for that hectic week-end in a cottage on the top of the rock cliff.

Almost on all fours I achieved that climb, but was rewarded for the effort by her joyful welcome. We discussed the events of the day, marvelling equally at its success. Apparently there had been only one "regrettable incident," and a shameful one at that. She told me that a bogus photographer had entered with an assistant, assuring my landlord, who accosted him, that his attendance at the fête had been authorised by me. (Liar!) He then proceeded to persuade mothers, wives and sweethearts of men serving in the Forces to have photographs taken to send to their loved ones. The results he put into envelopes, sealed them and gave them to his clients with strict injunctions not to open them for two hours, when, by some mysterious process, the photographs would be finished. When the envelopes were opened they had found — blank pieces of black paper, for which they had paid handsomely. A diabolically clever hoax, for the two hours of waiting to see results gave ample time for these rogues to escape. All this money must now be reimbursed to those cheated people from our French funds. Disgusting. Maddening. Humiliating and utterly damnable. Under a summer moon my secretary and I deplored the evil sometimes found in human nature. In parting, she said:

"Oh, darling, wasn't it charming of Monsieur and Madame Paris to descend that awful precipice at the end of a long day to say good-bye to you! Their car was at the door and our president trying to hustle them into it to keep an important engagement in London. *He* funked the climb, so smoked a cigar luxuriously on the top terrace. But *they* insisted that they must make that final effort to thank you personally for all that you are doing to help France."

"I never saw them," I said.

Then the awful truth flashed into my tired brain. The

"foreign-looking gentleman" accompanied by a smartly dressed lady whom old Nanny had shooed away from my closed door — Monsieur and Madame Paris!

And all day I had been sweating my soul out to do honour to the French. . . .

I explained what must have happened, and my secretary stared at me for a split second with horror in her eyes. Then our legs gave way under us, and simultaneously we sank down upon a mossy bank and laughed weakly, hysterically, hopelessly, until the tears ran down our cheeks. It was awful enough to be funny, and I think that both of us had a vision of grim old Nanny, with her massive form and jutting chin, shooing our guest of honour and his wife from the door.

ISIS publish a wide range of books in large print, from fiction to biography. A full list of titles is available free of charge from the address below. Alternatively, contact your local library for details of their collection of ISIS large print books.

Details of ISIS complete and unabridged audio books are also available.

Any suggestions for books you would like to see in large print or audio are always welcome.

7 Centremead
Osney Mead
Oxford OX2 0ES
(01865) 250333

ISIS REMINISCENCE SERIES

The ISIS Reminiscence Series has been developed with the older reader in mind. Well-loved in their own right, these titles have been chosen for their memory-evoking content.

FRED ARCHER
The Cuckoo Pen
The Distant Scene
The Village Doctor

BRENDA BULLOCK
A Pocket With A Hole

WILLIAM COOPER
From Early Life

KATHLEEN DAYUS
All My Days
The Best of Times
Her People

DENIS FARRIER
Country Vet

WINIFRED FOLEY
Back to the Forest
No Pipe Dreams for Father

PEGGY GRAYSON
Buttercup Jill

JACK HARGREAVES
The Old Country

ISIS REMINISCENCE SERIES

MOLLIE HARRIS
A Kind of Magic

ANGELA HEWINS
The Dillen

ELSPETH HUXLEY
Gallipot Eyes

LESLEY LEWIS
The Private Life Of A Country House

JOAN MANT
All Muck, No Medals

BRIAN P. MARTIN
Tales of the Old Countrymen
Tales of Time and Tide

VICTORIA MASSEY
One Child's War

JOHN MOORE
Portrait of Elmbury

PHYLLIS NICHOLSON
Country Bouquet

GILDA O'NEILL
Pull No More Bines

VALERIE PORTER
Tales of the Old Country Vets
Tales of the Old Woodlanders

ISIS REMINISCENCE SERIES

SHEILA STEWART
Lifting the Latch

JEAN STONE & LOUISE BRODIE
Tales of the Old Gardeners

EDWARD STOREY
In Fen Country Heaven
Fen Boy First

NANCY THOMPSON
At Their Departing

MARRIE WALSH
An Irish Country Childhood

RODERICK WILKINSON
Memories of Maryhill

GENERAL NON-FICTION

RICHARD EARL OF BRADFORD
Stately Secrets

WILLIAM CASH
Educating William

CLIVE DUNN
Permission to Laugh

EMMA FORD
Countrywomen

LADY FORTESCUE
Sunset House

JOANNA GOLDSWORTHY
Mothers: Reflections by Daughters

PATRICIA GREEN, CHARLES COLLINGWOOD
& HEIDI NIKLAUS
The Book of The Archers

HELENE HANFF
Letter From New York

ANDREW & MARIA HUBERT
A Wartime Christmas

MARGARET HUMPHREYS
Empty Cradles

JAMES LEITH
Ironing John

LESLEY LEWIS
The Private Life Of A Country House

GENERAL NON-FICTION

PETER MARREN & MIKE BIRKHEAD
Postcards From the Country

DESMOND MORRIS
The Human Animal

PHYLLIS NICHOLSON
Country Bouquet

FRANK PEARCE
Heroes of the Fourth Service

DAVA SOBEL
Longitude

SHEILA STEWART
Ramlin Rose

JOANNA TROLLOPE
Britannia's Daughters

NICHOLAS WITCHELL
The Loch Ness Story